MURDER
AT
MUSKET
BEACH

MURDER AT MUSKET BEACH

by

Bernie Lee

DONALD I. FINE, INC.
New York

Library of Congress Cataloging-in-Publication Data

Lee, Bernie.
Murder at Musket Beach: a novel / by Bernie Lee.
p. cm.
ISBN 1-55611-171-1 (alk. paper)
I. Title.
PS3562.E3326M87   1989
813'.54—dc20   89-46027 CIP
Manufactured in the United States of America
10 9 8 7 6 5 4 3 2 1

Designed by Irving Perkins Associates

*To Helen—who put meat on the table
and the kids through school and gave
me time for this—my love and all.*

ACKNOWLEDGMENTS

I want to acknowledge the Oregon Writers Colony and its founding members, including Marlene Howard, Jean Auel, Gail Tycer, Doreen Gandy, and the late Lola Strong-Janes, for the help they give, knowing and unknowing, to writers in our corner of the world. And to the many authors who've come to OWC conferences to teach or preach—Don Berry, Walt Morey, Nan Phillips, and Martha Kay Renfro are names that leap right up— thank you for your wary guidance. Thanks also to Chief David Rouse of the Cannon Beach Police Department for his cooperation.

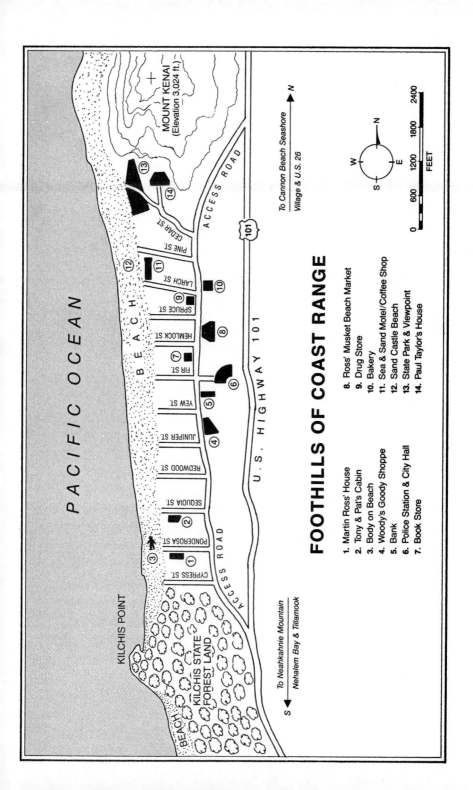

FOOTHILLS OF COAST RANGE

1. Martin Ross' House
2. Tony & Pat's Cabin
3. Body on Beach
4. Woody's Goody Shoppe
5. Bank
6. Police Station & City Hall
7. Book Store
8. Ross' Musket Beach Market
9. Drug Store
10. Bakery
11. Sea & Sand Motel/Coffee Shop
12. Sand Castle Beach
13. State Park & Viewpoint
14. Paul Taylor's House

MURDER
AT
MUSKET
BEACH

CHAPTER

ONE

Tuesday Evening— The Cabin at Musket Beach

"God, but I'm sick of murder!"

Hunched over the kitchen sink, Tony Pratt's not-quite-six-foot frame looked heavier than 180 pounds His voice was loud, almost a shout above the racket of cold water running hard into the metal sink.

Behind him, his wife turned and her brown eyes flashed a calculating look at him before she went on with opening a bottle of Chardonnay. "You say that every time," Pat said. She gave the metal corkscrew another twist and watched its levers lift up along its sides.

"I'm sick of murder and killing and I'm sick of hiding bodies and . . ."

"You say that *every* time. Look." Pat tilted her head

1

and her short, salt-and-pepper hair swung lightly against the cowl of her persimmon-colored sweater as she eyed the round-topped corkscrew standing in the bottle. "It looks like a little man. And when I twist his head, he lifts his little arms."

"But you enjoy it, don't you? You like the scheming, the plotting, the playing with people . . . damn! This water's cold!"

Pat shrugged. "Turn it off."

He turned it off.

"You've been scrubbing there for fifteen minutes," she said. "If you clean that crab any more, you'll rub right through the shell." Crouching to hold the bottle between the knees of her jeans with her left hand, she grabbed the corkscrew top in her right hand, pulled, gave a little grunt, and popped the cork. "Crack it and let's eat," and she took the wine and two glasses into the beach cabin's living-dining-and-sometimes-guest room.

"I'm serious!" he said.

"I know you're serious! And I'm hungry!" She came back into the kitchen. "So let's talk about your murders while we eat," she said, reaching up to pat his cheek. "Crusty French bread and expensive wine and delicious Dungeness crab—all paid for, incidentally, by those murders you're so sick of."

"*I* know they pay off. I can *see* they make money. But I *feel* that I could do something else—maybe even something a little more worthwhile."

Pat picked up the bowl of cold crab. "This," she said, smiling, "is quite worthwhile. Let's eat."

2

So they ate. And they talked. All through dinner, and part of another bottle of Chardonnay, doing the dishes, they talked about murder. They talked about schemes and plots, about some of the weird characters they had known, and about some of the eerie situations that Tony's work sometimes got them into. And they talked about how Tony would truly like to write something besides murder mysteries. Then they went for a walk on the beach and found the body.

TWO

Tuesday Night—
The Beach

WELL. To say that Tony and Pat "found" the body implies that they went looking for it, which is far from the fact. The fact is, if they had known that a body was sprawled there on the south end of Musket Beach, they would have gone north. Like a shot. They'd've run screaming for the cops. Cop, actually, because there was just one policeman per shift in this little town on Oregon's north coast.

No, they came across the body as a simple, direct result of all that wine.

Although they remembered to take a pocket flashlight for their walk on the beach, both husband and wife forgot how quickly the Pacific Ocean cools a summer breeze. So they went from the warm cabin into the starry First-of-July night wearing only sunny-day clothing against the chill wind off the sea. The result was that—midway through the fifty-yard walk to the bank overlooking the beach—Tony shivered, suddenly aware that he should have made a rest stop a long time ago. And scrambling down the rocky bank to the beach didn't help.

Then they walked south along the beach, skirting the roaring water's edge. As they walked, they watched the incoming tide splash and roll, the star-bright breakers foam and fall. Tony saw the ocean reaching closer and closer on the sand, and he became more and more conscious of the endless, ceaseless, insistent sound of running water.

"I have really got to go!" he said.

Pat stopped. Looking up at the sparkling stars, she stretched her arms wide and spoke to the sky. "And thank you for my husband, one of the last of the great romantics."

"Later, later." Tony was checking for other people up and down the beach: three or four families around campfires, a couple of couples walking along the water's edge, a jogger and her dog, all in the distance. "Nobody around."

He backed away from Pat, toward the bank, pointing in that direction. Over the surf sound she heard him say something about "... by the bank" and "... big piece of driftwood ... wait here!" He turned and shuffled quickly through the soft sand.

Pat loked after him for a moment before starting on down the beach. Then she stopped again.

"What big piece of driftwood?" she asked herself. "There was no driftwood when we walked along here after lunch. We even talked about how clear the beach was. And the tide's been out all afternoon. So how could there be driftwood?"

She looked after him again. Squinting, she just barely made out his dark silhouette in front of the even darker salal-covered bank. He stood, head tilted down, beside what appeared to be a log. Suddenly he jumped straight up, arms shooting out to the sides, made a mid-air turn, and plowed through the sand toward her.

Beyond Tony, and above, the darkness splintered as a pair of headlights flashed on. A car parked at road's end on the crest of the bank backed quickly away, its tires churning the gravel road so hard that thick clouds of dust bloomed up and seemed to dim the lights.

Pat started toward Tony.

The car made a violent stop-and-go U-turn in the narrow road, sending the sound of its grinding, whining gears over the noise of the surf. Its headlights tore a swinging arc across the dark fronts of houses and cabins and into the sky as it raced up the short hillside and into a screeching, tilting left turn onto the highway.

Through the dust that the car had kicked up on the little side road, a houselight came on.

On the beach, Tony stood in front of Pat, puffing a little, eyes wide, surprised, odd, his hands grabbing her shoulders.

"You must have put on quite a show," she said, half smiling. "What did you do?"

He shook his head quickly, several times, almost

7

like a shiver. "You won't believe this." His muttered words ran together. "There's a body back there."

"Not now! That 'somebody' just drove away."

"Not *some* body. *A* body. Look." He grabbed her hand and pulled her through the sand.

They stared down the flashlight's narrow yellow beam at the driftwood log. It was neatly dressed in short-sleeved shirt, slacks, socks, and wingtip oxfords. A long, slender, balding head topped the long, slender lifeless body. He lay as though he had been literally dumped on the sand, head turned to the ocean, body to the land, left arm pinned underneath. His right arm reached for the sea; his feet pointed left, as though walking away from it.

Pat shivered and looked away, toward the moon-white breakers.

Tony clicked the flashlight off but in that split second he caught a bright, metallic glint in the sand between the wingtip shoes. Crouching on one knee, he quickly combed the fingers of his right hand through the sand. They closed around a narrow, flat, metal rectangle.

When he stood up, Pat exhaled a deep, deep breath. "You're sure he's dead?" she asked.

Tony put an arm around his wife's shoulders and said, "He was in the same position when I first saw him. That's a long time to hold a pose."

"But have you touched him?" She looked everywhere but at that thing on the sand—at the sea, at the sky, at anything else, but not the body. Her left arm wrapped around Tony's waist, her right reached in front of her, seeming to search; her head swung from side to side in the rhythm of her questions, "Is he warm? Is he cold? Is he shot? Is he . . ."

She gasped and stopped as another blinding light exploded down from the bank above.

"What's happening there on the beach!" a man shouted from behind the light. "Are you people all right?"

Pat and Tony twisted away from the light, trying to shield their eyes. She raised her hands to her face. He held his left forearm up to block the light while he dropped the small piece of metal into the right-hand pocket of his slacks.

"Who're you!" Tony yelled back, "and get that light out of our face!"

"Musket Beach Police! What's wrong with that man!"

"We don't know! We just found him!"

"Just *found* . . . ?"

The light jerked away, skittered down through the shiny dark salal on the bank, and jounced across the few feet of sand with surprising speed, slicing quick long lines in the dark. It stopped on the body. Tony and Pat stood silent, watching the police officer—young, about Tony's height, thinner—shine his light slowly along the length of the corpse.

"Well I'll be damned!" he said, and dropped to one knee beside the body. He felt first for a heartbeat, then for a pulse in the carotid artery.

"You know him?" Tony asked.

"Cool," the officer said. "Not cold. But cool. Well, I'll be damned."

"You know him?" asked Pat.

Carefully, the officer laid the bulb end of his heavy-duty flashlight against the lifeless cheek and turned the lifeless head. A long, bruised ridge bulged over the right temple; a thin strand of dried blood stretched from the bulge almost to the ear. Pat and Tony saw the blood and sucked air in sharply, together.

"Well. I'll be damned."

The policeman pulled the flashlight away. The head rolled back, facing the sea again. Pat and Tony glanced at each other, wincing.

As the officer stood, he tugged his two-way radio out of its holster on his left hip and made two calls—one for the deputy medical examiner and the other for an ambulance from the emergency medical station in Seashore Village, fifteen miles north. The end of his call for the ambulance was almost an afterthought. "Make this one a Code Two."

Pat looked a question at Tony, who said, "Code Two tells the driver to use the overhead flashing lights, but not the siren. In other words: Hurry, but don't break any records."

While he talked, he watched the officer's light move around the body and over the sand alongside. It paused at a spot between the shoes. The officer squatted, looking closely at the sand. "Have either of you touched the body?"

10

Pat shook her head.

"No," said Tony.

"Or anything else?"

Tony shook his head.

Pat said, "No."

Standing again, the officer moved his light on to where Tony and Pat stood.

Once again Tony asked, "Do you know him?"

"Yes," the officer said, and raised his light to shine it waist-high between Pat and Tony, not high enough for them to flinch from the glare but high enough to read their faces clearly. "I know *him.* But I don't know *you.*"

"Well, hell, Barrett, they're all right!"

At the loud voice from the darkness, all three of them jumped and Officer Barrett roared. "Jee-zus H. Christ!" He spun around toward the bank and his flashlight picked out a short, stout figure crossing the dark sand. Its arms shot up to ward off the glare, scrunching an unzipped rain parka over a pajama top and a bare round belly. Pajama legs hung below corduroy jeans and drooped around bare ankles and old-fashioned leather bedroom slippers with elastic at the instep.

"Now *I've* got to," Pat said.

"What the hell're you *doin'* here, Martin?" Barrett spoke roughly, but he lowered his light for Martin Ross, owner of the Musket Beach Market.

Tony looked at Pat sympathetically, "You mean, you've got to . . . ?"

11

She nodded. "Bad!" she said, shifting her weight.

"You know these people?" Barrett asked Ross.

Flashlight reflections bounced on and off Ross round, rimless glasses as he twisted and jerked his head around to look at the officer, at Pat, at Tony, and quickly at Pat again before turning back to Officer Barrett. His hands and arms jerked around, too; patting his belly, pushing his glasses up, checking his fly, wiping his palms on the seat of his pants. "To answer your first question, Barrett, about what I'm doing here," the grocer said, "I live right up there." He waved toward the road where the light had come on. Then he added in a slightly sarcastic tone, "You oughta know that, Barry—how long you been wearin' that badge around here? Three years? Four?" He peered through his glasses at the policeman for a long second before going on.

"Second, Mr. and Mrs. Pratt here—Tony and Pat— he's a writer and she's a Financial Consultant." His head cocked toward the Pratts and he jerked a thumb over his shoulder. "They bought the old Tyler cabin on the next road north, about a block from my house." Ross looked sharply at Barrett again. "You oughta know *that,* too."

"Well," Tony said, "it's just a little place. Sort of a hideaway place." Barrett gave him a funny look, so he added, "We live in Portland and use the beach place for weekends, holidays, vacations."

"They been comin' to Musket Beach and buyin' groceries in my store for more'n a year, so o' course I know Mr. and Miz Pratt . . . 'n' that's that."

Barrett raised one eyebrow and looked at Pat. "Your name is really Pat? Pat Pratt?"

"Never mind," Pat groaned, shifting back and forth from foot to foot

"Third," Ross hurried on "I say we let Miz Pratt retire to my house" And to Pat he said, "The one with lights on"

Tony handed her the flashlight and, without a word, she hurried toward the dark, narrow path up the bank as Ross called after her "Through the livingroom, first door on the right!"

"Hey!" Officer Barrett yelped. "I can't let her leave!"

The other two men just looked at him.

The little light bobbed rapidly away

THREE

Tuesday Night—
The Beach (continued)

BARRETT sighed.

"Okay," he said, "let's get back to my *first* question, Martin. What *are* you doin' here?"

"Well, I was gettin' ready for bed," Ross said. "But a car started gunnin' back and forth on my road up there. I got to the window just as it come tearin' past my place and on down the highway. So I stood there for a little bit, lookin' out, wonderin' if there was any more weirdos around. Then *you* come by." Ross winked at Tony and grunted. "Funny coincidence, huh?" He turned back to Barrett. "Sorta wondered why you didn't take out after that guy."

He paused, waiting for Barrett to say something. When the officer just stood there, watching him, Ross went on with his story. "But you just came on down the road and stopped and got out and stood there on the bank, shinin' your light down to the beach. And then you all-of-a-sudden hustled down the bank, so I pulled my pants and coat on and come along to see what's what." He paused again. "So that's that." He paused a third time, before saying softly, "Except for whatever it is on the ground right there that nobody's talkin' about."

Barrett lowered his arm and clicked on his flash. Light struck the wingtip shoes on the sand.

Ross looked down and when he saw the shoes he gave a sudden grunt and stepped back as though he'd been hit in the belly. He blinked several times at the body. He didn't say anything for nearly half a minute, and when he spoke he sounded almost cautious and his voice broke once. "What's the matter with . . . with our leading man? . . . with our mayor?"

"Mayor!" Tony said.

Ross' voice was almost a moan, barely audible over the surf. "Lordy, lordy, what have we done?"

As though he hadn't heard Martin Ross's sad comment, Officer Barrett said, "He's dead." Then he whipped his light back up to Ross' chest and snapped, "How'd you know it was Conley?"

"What happened to him?"

"Looks like somebody whopped him alongside the head," the officer said. "Now listen to me, Martin. You don't own this town *yet,* so you answer me! How'd you know it was Carl Conley?"

Ross took a deep breath before he finally looked

at Barrett and pointed to the wingtips and said, "Well, hell, Barry, who else around here wears shoes like that?—like some hotshot, big-town real estate broker? Nobody but our own hotshot, small-town big-dealer."

"Wait a minute," Tony said. "You said something about 'leading man.' Is this the mayor? Or some actor? Or some real estate guy?"

"Both," said Officer Barrett.

"All," said Ross. "One and the same. Bein' mayor of Musket Beach is just about a one-hour job. That is, if you take your time..."

"And a long lunch," Barrett put in.

"Our current mayor," Ross continued, motioning toward the body, "that is, our late mayor, Carl Conley—he was very big in the local Little Theater. But his main business was real estate. You see his signs all over the county. Drawing of a bird? Big white bird?"

"And the name of the company?" Barrett added. "Good Tern Realty?"

Tony nodded and smiled. "Well, anybody who can think of a name like that can't be all bad."

"You got it," the officer said.

"Got what?"

"Conley didn't think of that name."

"It didn't belong to him no more than a lot o' things he claimed," Martin Ross added, his voice scornful and rasping, "includin' that woman who's *supposed* to be his *wife*. His *second* wife. 'n' that's that."

*　*　*

Except for the surf—nearer, now, with the rising tide—this bit of beach lay silent in the moonlight.

Officer Barrett got a blanket from his car and covered the body. After that the three men stood, around the body but each apart, looking out to sea.

Tony touched the long, thin metal rectangle in his pocket, fingers feeling the odd grooves on its top, thumb rubbing the rough trace of some kind of adhesive on the bottom. At one point he came close to handing it over to Officer Barrett; he opened his mouth and turned to speak and found the policeman watching him, almost expectantly. Tony turned back to the sea and said nothing.

Then came the tinkling sound of a dog's license clinking on its collar; its owner's jogging feet thudded on the hard, wet sand; a string of pre-Fourth fire-crackers flashed and rattled at one of the far campfires; the dog snuffled busily around the blanket; the ambulance arrived and rolled down the little road to stop at the bank-top, red and blue lights spinning stark, ripping circles through the night over their heads; the jogger hurried into the group and grabbed her dog's collar; a spotlight on the ambulance burned a brilliant white cone of light down to the beach, changing the sand to snow and shaping squat black shadows beside everything it touched.

Coming back from Martin Ross' house, Pat found the bright yellow ambulance blocking the path down the bank. She stood beside the hot throbbing engine, ignoring the fumes and noise, and looked down at the three men standing around the blanket, their forms and shadows distorted by the angle and the light.

One man turned his head in her direction. The spotlight glinted off his glasses and made them opaque, two round white spots burned in a big round head. Flashing at her from the beach, their blank glare shook Pat with a sharp, intuitive jolt, and she knew. And from the way that he stood, head turned, unmoving, staring up at her, Pat knew that he knew. Somehow she sensed that, behind those blind-looking glasses, Martin Ross was remembering the note, remembering that he'd left it there on his desk, in plain sight. And he knew that she'd seen it.

Pat concentrated next on Tony. Looking down at him, in that eerie scene on the beach below, she wondered, "How does he feel about murder *now?*"

FOUR

Tuesday Night— The Cabin

IT was past midnight when Officer Barrett asked his last question "for the time being." Martin Ross and the ambulance people and even the jogger with her dog had answered his questions on the cool, suddenly-windy beach. But Tony had insisted on getting Pat back to the warmth of the cabin.

Now, two hours later, over wine for themselves and root beer for Barrett, they were discovering that he was a very thorough police officer when he made out his reports. Finally, he flipped his notebook shut and started hoisting himself off the stool at the counter between the kitchen and dining room.

"Before you go," Tony said, "would it be all right to ask *you* a couple of questions?"

"Sure," Barrett said, settling back again. "What's on your mind?"

"Down there on the beach, when Martin Ross saw the body—when he realized who it was—remember what he said?"

Barrett's mouth curled down as he thought for a second or two before shaking his head. "No," he said, with a question on the end of it.

"'Lordy, lordy,'" Tony quoted the grocer. "Remember that? 'Lordy, lordy, what have we done?'"

Pat nodded, and finally Barrett did, too. "Oh, yeah. He did say something like that—like he was prayin' or something."

"What do you suppose he meant by that: 'What have we done?'"

"*Meant* by it? Nothing. As I said, it was kind of like a prayer."

Pat looked at Tony, then at Barrett. "Is he a religious person?"

"Well, more'n a lot of us, I guess," Barrett said with half a grin. "He goes to church fairly regular, but he doesn't make a big deal out of it. Guess it's in his background." The officer paused, looking carefully at Tony and Pat. "Martin's a good person. You can tell by his manner. It's just that sometimes he acts like he thinks he bought the whole town when he bought that store. But he's okay." Barrett leaned forward again, about to get up. "Anything else?"

"One more thing," Tony said. "Somebody said—either you or Ross—somebody said something about a 'leading man.'"

22

Barrett's head jerked back as he gave a silent laugh. "That was Martin. Martin said that."

"What was that all about?"

The expression on Barrett's face was half-frown, half-smile as he said, "Sometimes Martin gets—*used* to get on Carl's case for years 'cause Carl always wanted to be an actor. Never got over his 'Little Theater' days in Portland. That's how Carl got to Musket Beach in the first place, as I understand it."

Pat frowned. "What do you mean? As an actor? Here?"

"As I say . . ." Barrett shrugged. "The way I understand it is, the lady that ran the Musket Beach Little Theater saw him in a play in Portland and offered him a summer job here. I guess he was runnin' out of 'Little Theater' parts to play in Portland so he jumped at it. But if you ask me, he was gettin' kind of long in the tooth for that kind of stuff."

Barrett's shoulders moved with another silent laugh.

Her voice quiet, Pat asked, "How old was he, do you know?"

"Carl? About fifty, I'd say. Been here ten years or so. So he must've been about forty when she made the offer. Anyway, he jumped at it." Barrett grinned. "Jumped at the lady, too, they say. Married her. That's how he got into the real estate business. She owned it. A real boomer, she must have been; the best real estate agent on the coast, people say. Then she had a heart attack and died about three years ago and Carl took over and the whole thing's been slidin' downhill ever since." Barrett's head wagged back and forth a couple of times. "Even so, it was always like Carl was 'on' all the time, always acting—almost like he was in a play or something."

After a second or two of silence, Tony said, "From what Martin Ross said, I gather that he married again."

Barrett's mouth and mustache started to twitch around his grin. "Yeah, he got married, alrighty."

"Well, did his second wife help with the business?"

This time Barrett's laugh was a loud bark. "Har! CarolMae?" He barked again and then went on in a mocking tone, "Pardon me: 'Carole, with an "e",' as she calls herself now." Barrett couldn't seem to stop grinning. "No, I don't think CarolMae Arp was much help to Carl with the real estate business."

Pat was looking at him sharply. "You seem to know her very well."

Barrett laid a big hand across the top of his root beer can and started tilting it back and forth on the counter. His voice became serious and quiet. "CarolMae and me? We go 'way back." He jerked his head to the east. "Back over these mountains, in fact. We grew up in the same little tiny town just this side of Jewel. She was two or three years behind me in high school." He stopped for a second and smiled, mostly to himself. "Actually, CarolMae was a couple of years behind me in *school* but about twenty years ahead in everything else, if you know what I mean."

The officer looked at Pat and at Tony before he picked up his root beer, drained the last two swallows, and put the can down again. "CarolMae's daddy was a logger and her mama tended bar at that big tavern on the highway and she got out o' that scene as quick as she could. Quit high school, in fact. Started waitressin'. Fryin' hamburgers at joints along the highway. Sort of workin' her way over here to the coast. CarolMae kept watchin' folks drive by in their Mercedes or their Volvo or their BMW, comin' to their beach houses. I guess she thought the whole coast was like that and she wanted herself a little taste of it. But when she got here she found out it wasn't quite like that."

Barrett sat motionless for several seconds, looking down at the cabin floor. "She was workin' at Woody's Goody Shoppe here in Musket Beach when she met Carl." Still looking down he said, almost to himself, "Ever since she was a little girl CarolMae always wanted something that was a little farther off than she could grab. Maybe when she married Carl, even though he was old enough to be her daddy, maybe she thought she was gettin' it. But now?—who knows what she's after?" He paused, then looked up and said loudly, "But that's enough for tonight, folks. Or, as Martin Ross would say, 'That's that.'"

Barrett stood, adjusted his creaking belt and holster, cautioned the Pratts against leaving Musket Beach without stopping at the police station, gave them directions to the station, belched, and left.

As Tony locked the front door behind Barrett, he looked at Pat. She was leaning forward in the rocker by the wood stove, head down, elbows on knees, fingers stretched through her hair.

"Quite a story," he said, coming back from the door.

Sitting up, letting the chair rock back, Pat put her feet on the polished hatchcover coffee table. She nodded, eyes closed. "Quite a night, too. Sure glad the kids aren't here. I'd hate to have them go through this."

He sat on the table beside her crossed ankles. "Oh, they'd handle it all right." He lifted her feet slightly, slid over, and let them rest on his knees.

"I'm not sure *I'm* handling it all right," she said with a sigh. "So I don't know how a couple of college kids would do."

"You're doing fine." He untied her sneakers and took them off. Holding one small foot in each hand, he gently massaged her insteps with his thumbs.

Moments passed.

"Nice," Pat said, eyes still closed.

"Good."

A few more moments, then Tony said, "I think I'll have a glass of wine, how about you?"

"Please."

"Then we should go to bed."

"Yes," she said, shifting her feet so he could get up.

Her deep brown eyes were open, red-rimmed and veined, when he came back with two filled glasses.

"You know what's really scary?" Pat asked, reaching up and taking hers by the stem. "What's really scary is, there's someone in this quiet little beach town crazy enough to kill somebody."

He looked down at her, her head almost lost in the cowl collar of her sweater. "Maybe that someone isn't crazy," Tony said in a wondering tone. "Maybe that someone is desperate. Or angry. Or scared. Or—"

He shrugged and stopped. His right hand, almost automatically, slipped into his pocket and around the piece of flat metal.

"You sound like a man trying to work out a plot," she said.

After a second he nodded, "I guess you're right."

Taking the piece out of his pocket, he sat again on the edge of the coffee table.

Pat raised her glass for a toast.

"Well, here's to *not* working out a real, *live* murd— what's that!" she said, surprised at seeing the shining metal.

"I'm not sure," Tony answered.

"You're not sure? Where'd it come from?"

Again she raised her glass to sip as Tony said, "By the body."

She almost choked. "By the *body*!"

Her shaking glass dribbled wine and rattled when she put it on the table. She stared at him as she rubbed distractedly at several drops on her jeans and looked at her husband. Still not believing, she now almost whispered, "You found it by the *body*?"

"Between his feet."

She shook her head slowly, staring at him. "And you just picked it up? And kept it?"

"I've seen these things before. Somewhere."

"Let me see."

She held the little rectangle of metal with her thumbs and forefingers at the corners, turned it, examined it: narrow and flat, about five inches long, maybe an inch wide and a quarter-of-an-inch thick;

grooves and slits on the long, flat top; slick and smooth all over, except for a rough spot on the bottom, as though it had been stuck to something and pulled loose; no identifying mark or symbol or name.

"Looks like it was glued to something else," she said.

"I noticed that."

Pat looked at the piece a little longer before she said, "You're serious? You didn't show it to the police? To Officer Barrett?"

Tony shook his head.

"I started to say something to him, two or three times." He shrugged. "But I couldn't. I don't know why. I guess I thought maybe I could help, maybe figure something out, if I held onto it." He swallowed a little wine. "Or maybe I thought it might have nothing to do with the body, that maybe it was there before the body was." Again he shook his head. "I don't know."

"I don't know either, Tony, but I suspect Barrett would consider it evidence. And look at the way we've been handling it. Our fingerprints must be all over it. We've probably messed up any other prints that were there."

He took the piece back. "Could be. But if any prints were on it they were probably messed up by the sand. And if it was in the sand before the body was put there, it has nothing to do with this. And besides, I'm not sure metal like this takes good prints."

She looked down at her hands, clasped between her knees, then back at Tony. "You're feeling pretty guilty about not turning this thing over to Barrett, aren't you?"

He drained the last of his wine and carried the glass into the kitchen and put it in the sink. "I was," he said from the kitchen. "But not now." Coming back into the livingroom, he was lightly tossing and catching the thin little silver block. "Because first thing tomorrow," he paused and glanced at his watch, "later today, that is, I'll take it to Barrett and tell all."

Looking at Tony, Pat's eyes flared wide open for an instant. She sat straight up, shoulders squared, before she glanced away, then back at him, and away again.

Tony stood without moving, clutching the piece of metal in his right hand, watching her. "What's wrong?"

Pat said nothing. The long quiet was underlined by a noise outside, like the wind brushing against the cabin.

When she finally looked at Tony again, with serious, worried eyes, she still held her shoulders square and sat straight up. "There's something I haven't told you, yet, and I don't know why, except that I didn't want to say anything about it there on the beach with those other people around. And when we came back here it kept jumping in and out of my mind. And then Barrett came in and it didn't seem to be the right time to talk about it "

Pat slumped back into the rocker, seeming to be a little embarrassed, as always, when she forgot about something she thought he'd want to know.

She scrunched around in the chair and straightened her right leg so she could dig into the pocket of her jeans. Pulling out a scrap of crumpled paper, she told him about the note she'd seen on Martin Ross' desk.

29

"Right after we found the body, remember? When I went up to Martin Ross' house to use the bathroom?" Animated again, she rocked forward and opened the piece of paper on the table, trying to press out the wrinkles with the flat of her hand.

"Well, his desk is in the living room. I had to walk right past it on my way to the john. And coming back, too. So on my way out I just sort of *glanced* at the stuff spread all over the top of his desk, you know, the way people do . . ."

"Naturally."

". . . and there was this note that seemed to jump up off the desk at me. Because of that funny word, I guess."

"What funny word?" Tony moved around and sat down on the table, craning his neck sideways to look at Pat's piece of paper.

"Guru."

"Guru?"

"See? Wouldn't it catch *your* eye, a note with 'guru' in it?" She held up the paper. Tony took it with one hand as he put the metal piece down with the other. "So I copied it. So you could see it exactly the way I saw it. Punctuation and all."

Tony read it aloud to himself. "'Martin, Guru says OK!' With a bang-mark."

He looked at Pat with a quick expression that turned his mouth down and wrinkled his chin for a second. "And it's signed 'CC'."

"I wonder if that could be Carl Conley?" Pat asked.

30

"Could be." He thought for a second. "Or *Carole* Conley?"

Pat's eyebrows shot up for a second and she nodded. "Could be. But do you see why it caught my eye?" Before Tony could answer, she added, "What's a bang-mark?"

"Exclamation point. I've heard advertising art directors call it that, sometimes. Typesetters, too, sometimes."

"Makes it sound really important, doesn't it: 'Martin. Guru says okay. Bang!'"

Tony nodded. "Makes it a lot more emphatic."

"Almost triumphant, even."

"As though somebody had worked very hard for something they didn't expect to win."

Pat relaxed back into the rocker again, stretching. "Well, I suppose we should tell Officer Barry Barrett about—" and suddenly she was yawning, and speaking through the yawn "—excuse me, tell Barrett about the note *and* that piece of metal."

Tony took her hands, helping her to stand. "This has been a long, strange, wearing day," he said, sliding his hands up her arms to her shoulders. "Time to put it behind us."

She rested her head on his chest. "I'm not sure I can," she said softly, and yawned again.

"We can try," he said, guiding her toward the bedroom with his left arm around her shoulders. His right hand flicked off the light switch as they passed.

Behind them the bright livingroom dropped away,

leaving a dark space touched here and there by stray rays of pinkish light wandering down through occasional gaps in the curtains from the only light on their road—the vapor lamp of a streetlight midway between the cabin and the path down the bank to the beach. One narrow shaft shone across the coffee table and onto the metal piece Tony had found. Its silver sheen was an almost perfect match for the gleam on Officer Barrett's badge when he turned from the corner window and started up the road toward his car.

FIVE

Wednesday Morning— The Cabin

SUMMER on the north Oregon coast offers a variety of weather. Usually, the choice is between Moist, Damp or Wet. Although springtime brings days of splendor and autumn can be glorious, Oregon's average summer day is best described as long and liquid.

Take the typical Fourth of July, for example. In the morning, people smile at the nice blue, puffy-cloud sky. At lunch they stir their bowls of chowder under a gray overcast. In late afternoon, the overcast drops around their ankles. At dinnertime everybody wears rain parkas and wool hats and wonders about getting out of the house for some fresh air.

And at dusk, when the Musket Beach Volunteer Fire Department lights up its Annual Fireworks Display all those noisy, colorful, booming, popping, patriotic fizgigs turn into dull thuds and pale pastels. A thick, soggy wall of fog sucks up that sharp explosive smell and holds it in front of your nose; you can almost grab a handful and stuff it in your parka pocket.

On Oregon's north coast, that sort of day is classified as Moist.

Damp and Wet aren't nearly so nice.

On this July 2nd, though—the morning after finding the body—Tony stood on the front deck of his cabin, looked out at the ocean, and rated the day exceptional: Clear, cloudless sky; sun rising over the Coast Range warming his back; white-rimmed blue Pacific tumbling onto the beach; temperature in the 60s and rising. It was a meteorological phenomenon.

A high-pressure system had sneaked in during the night. It nudged the predicted low-pressure weather out of the way, either down to California or up to British Columbia, and settled over Oregon for a long stay. And good weather meant a lot of money for Musket Beach this weekend because it was Sand Castle Time.

Every year, the Chamber of Commerce scheduled Musket Beach Sand Castle Time on a weekend near the Fourth of July, depending on the ocean tides. This year the weekend fell smack on Independence Day, thanks to one of the lowest tides of the summer.

On Sand Castle weekend the little town of 850 was to put it mildly, loaded. From twenty- to twenty-five-

34

thousand tourists crunched in to see the competition, viewing as many as two hundred sand sculptures covering a quarter-mile of beach.

The first competition, organized more than twenty years ago, was started by a couple of mothers as "something for the kids to do" during summer vacations. Planning and building sand castles turned out to be so much fun that the big people barged in. Ordinarily, that's when the fun stops for the kids. But those mothers were smart and quick. They saw what was happening and set up age-group classifications to make sure that kids would compete against kids and grownups against grownups. So the contest stayed fun for everyone.

It must be. Top prize is ten dollars. But the contest draws hundreds of contestants across surprising distances. Families, couples, foursomes, church groups, clubs, fraternities, sororities—they come from all over Oregon, Idaho, California, Washington, and British Columbia to spend a long, shivering night on the beach shoveling and shaping the cold, heavy, wet sand into sometimes wondrous designs. A committee of local artists, gallery owners, and bartenders then judges the designs and awards prizes. After this, in unbelievable lines, thousands of tourists stroll, shuffle, or stagger by to gape at the artistry in the sand. There's usually at least one sea monster, huge and threatening; real sand castles, tall and fussily ornate; fishing boats named "May" or "Ginger"; a dog named Snoopy, a Long John Silver with real peg leg, and a Marilyn Monroe.

Sometime during all the gawking, a spectator feels

his feet getting wet. He announces, with a definite slur in his speech, "The tide is turning." All the tourists then move slowly up the beach, away from the sculptures, toward their cars. That leaves the sand sculptors—the artists of the day—who gather in intimate little clusters around their work and watch the tide, wave by wave, wash it all away.

So. When good weather holds through the Fourth of July weekend, tourist business booms in the local shops and restaurants, at the gas station and the grocery store. Then, given another busy weekend over Labor Day, summer ends for Musket Beach with money in the bank.

Finally, when the last tourist leaves, the little town battens down for another cold, wet, wind-driven winter. And the locals, comfortable once again with their own 850 souls, happily slosh back and forth trading summer dollars among themselves, until spring flashes green again with another crop of tourists.

Tony, musing about these things to avoid thinking about the other thing, finally took a deep breath and went back into the cabin to dial Officer Barrett's telephone number.

The phone rang twice. The line clicked four times. After the clicking came a long *hummm* overlaid by an electronic jingling tune followed by the sound of someone snapping his fingers followed by paper rattling followed by two quick coughs, followed by a man's scratchy, hollow, recorded voice saying, with self-conscious formality, "Thank you for calling the Musket Beach Police Department. All personnel are otherwise occupied. When you hear the tone, please state the date, the time, your name, your purpose in calling, and your telephone number. An officer will contact you as soon as . . ."

The recorded message clicked off and the phone rattled and banged before a woman's smoke-husky voice said, in the distance, ". . . dropped the goddamn thing." Then she came on straight into Tony's ear, "Hello! I mean, City Hall! I mean, Police Department!"

"What was that? The police department has a telephone answering machine?"

Without inflection, the husky voice said, "No, it belongs to the liberry. What can I do for you."

"I'm calling Officer Barrett. Is he in?"

"If there was anybody over there would I answer this phone? No." A rustling noise came over the line as she shifted the receiver. "Hold it. I seen a note stuck up here somewhere. Yeah. Here. Says, 'Worked late—be in about eleven. Barry.'"

"That's from Officer Barrett?"

"That's from Officer Barrett," the flat voice said. "Any message?"

"No, I'll just come by around eleven o'clock. But tell me," he added quickly, "why does the police department have an answering machine?"

"Because the cheap-ass voters in this town won't pay for more people," she said.

"Hey! How can you talk that way? You don't even know who I am!"

"Hmm. That's true. Well." There was a short cough, and for the first time the voice showed interest. "You know who I am?"

"No."

"Good."

The phone line clicked and died.

Pat, in her dark green robe, came from the kitchen carrying a steaming white coffee mug. She stopped at the door, watching Tony, who was staring at the dead receiver in his hand.

"Who doesn't know who you are?" she asked.

"I don't know."

She blew a long, gentle breath across the top of her coffee mug, then shrugged. "Sounds fair," she said, and went on out the door to the deck.

Tony blinked at the phone, hung it up, and went out to stand beside her.

"Hi," he said, touching her shoulder lightly, "I didn't realize you were up. Sleep all right?"

"Better than I expected, after last night. Still a bit shaky, though." She shivered. "Never, never, ever even imagined I would actually be involved in such a thing."

"I know," he said, giving her shoulder a little rub. "But our part in this will soon be over. I just tried to call Barrett—he's due at the police station around eleven o'clock. I'll drive in and turn that piece of metal and the note over to him and we'll be out of it."

"I hope so," Pat sighed.

38

"You'll see," he said. "Change of subject: What's for breakfast?"

Pat shivered again. "I don't know. I haven't even thought about it. What would you like?"

"Oh, I don't know. Waffles, maybe. Or how about Eggs Benedict?"

She turned her head and looked at him, thinking.

"Why is it," she asked calmly, "when it's *your* turn to cook we have very simple meals—cold cracked crab, for example, or take-and-bake pizza? But when it's *my* turn, you want something like Eggs Benedict or *Coquilles St. Jacques*—something that takes four hours and 87 pots and pans?"

"Funny how that works out, isn't it," Tony said, his eyes on a flight of five pelicans circling over the water just beyond the white line of breaking waves. "Probably some variation on Pratt's Laundry Law."

"Which is?"

"When it's *your* turn to do the laundry, the only things in the wash are blouses, underwear, and socks. But when it's *my* turn, I get not only blouses, underwear, and socks, but somehow every towel, dish towel, wash cloth, sheet, and pillowcase in the house needs washing."

Pat swirled the coffee in her cup and studied it for a moment before she spoke. "Scrambled eggs and raisin bread toast?"

"Sounds good," Tony said, watching a pelican suddenly fold its wings and dive into the sea for breakfast.

39

SIX

Wednesday Morning— The Musket Beach Police Station

At 11:05 Tony drove his gray Capri around to the two-car parking lot beside Musket Beach City Hall. The one-story building sat squat and square, its vertical cedar siding weathered to a silvery gray. A fake mansard roof, drooping low over its two widely-spaced windows and the double door in between, made it look like a frowning Buddha. But it was home to Musket Beach, Oregon's city government, plus the Chamber of Commerce, the fire truck, the police car, and the city jail.

Planted in front was a three-foot square redwood carving of the town's emblem: A crossed pair of flintlock guns, the kind with a short stubby barrel and flared muzzle. In 1863, one of those old blunderbusses was found in the sand of what has been known, from that moment on, as Musket Beach. How they appeared on the Oregon coast, nobody knows—possibly they fell overboard or washed up from the wreck of an eighteenth-century Dutch or Spanish or English explorer.

Another thing nobody knows is how another town about twenty miles north on the same coast could get away with copying Musket Beach. But there it is, a Johnny-come-lately in Oregon history called Cannon Beach.

Climbing out of his Capri, Tony found himself wishing that Carl Conley's body were a problem for Cannon Beach instead of Musket Beach. Shaking that idea out of his head, he dropped his keys into the left-hand pocket of his red windbreaker, hitched up his jeans, and walked the gravel path along the side of the building, following directions from a red wooden arrow nailed to the back corner. Behind the building, another "Police" arrow led him through a scuffed, tan-painted doorway. He took three steps along a trail worn in the pink linoleum and looked across a counter at the Musket Beach Police Department.

There were two rooms. The smaller one, probably six feet wide and eight feet long, was to his left, through an open door with a Yale lock and a sign that said "Holding Room." In the room Tony could see only an opened rollaway bed with a bare, yellow-stained mattress.

The larger room was about eight-by-twelve feet.

Four of the twelve feet, cut off by the counter, formed the little reception area where Tony stood now, along with a low table and a chair. On the wall, fifteen wanted posters were push-pinned to an old, chewed-up cork bulletin board.

In the middle of the main room, nearly lost under a cloud of papers, two tiny gray metal desks butted together. Two metal folding chairs looked at each other across the desks. A low shelf on the right wall ran the length of the plywood-paneled room, interrupted halfway along by a small window. The shelf seemed to stagger under the weight of brown cardboard filing cases, wire baskets filled with pink, blue, and green forms, a red-and-white plastic lunch cooler, a tall thermos bottle, a steel-string guitar, and a two-way radio with its red "On" light on and its speaker alternately squawking and silent.

Centered in the far wall was a double-locked door. Through its clear glass window, Tony saw a few City Hall employees moving around or working at their desks. But here in the cop shop, there was no one at home.

So he jumped a little when Officer Barrett said loudly, "You like your coffee black? Or milk or sugar or both or what?" and poked his head out the doorway of the Holding Room.

Surprised, Tony's answer was just as loud. "Black! Black's fine."

Barrett laughed and said, "Good. I'm out of all that other stuff, anyway." He walked carefully into the larger room holding a white Styrofoam cup in each hand. Watching the cups, he nodded toward a hip-high wooden gate hung on the end of the counter. "Come on in.'

"How did you know I was here?" Tony pushed through and let the gate thump shut behind him.

"Saw you through the window when I got up to get myself a cup. Figured you'd prob'ly have one, too."

Barrett offered a coffee cup to Tony and at the same time toed one of the metal folding chairs around to the side of his desk. Gesturing toward the chair, he settled into his own, his leather belt and holster squeaking.

"Now," he said, raising his cup as Tony eased into the metal chair, "what's on your mind?" He slurped the hot coffee. His face squinched up and the steam disappeared into his pursed mustache, but his narrowed eyes stayed focused on Tony.

Tony hoisted his cup, then put it on the desk without drinking. He reached into the right-hand pocket of his jacket as a brief, embarrassed smile flowed across his face. "There's something I should have told you last night," he said, "something I should have given you. A *couple* of things, in fact." He took out the small metal rectangle and stood it on its side on the desk. "I found this on the beach last night. By the body."

Barrett didn't look down. Instead, he kept looking at Tony, a satisfied gleam lighting his eyes. "To tell you the truth, I kinda *knew* you had something. Or had something you wanted to *say*."

Finally he looked at the piece of metal.

"What is it? And why didn't you speak up?"

Tony hesitated. "I wanted to. I *started* to. But for some reason I held back. I still don't know why." He leaned back, shaking his head. "And I'm not sure what that piece of metal is."

There was a jittery kind of silence. Barrett stared at Tony. A shrill, raucous ring from the telephone on Barrett's desk broke the spell. Without looking away, the officer fingered through the paper mess on his desk and pressed a button on the answering machine by the phone. A red light popped on and the machine began to whir, taking the call.

Barrett set his coffee down and picked up the metal piece. "I'll give you some good advice," Barrett said, not looking at Tony but at the block. "Odd-lookin' thing."

Then he looked at Tony. "Some good advice. And I'm serious. Don't hold back again. Even if you don't know what you've got."

He paused for a deep breath just as the answering machine clicked off, and before he could start again, Tony interrupted. "There's something else," he said. Pulling Pat's scrap of paper out of his pocket, he held it out to the officer.

"Now what's *this?*" Barrett reached across the desk and took it.

"A note that my wife saw."

"'Martin. Guru says OK! CC.'" He blinked a couple of times and shook his head. "What *is* that? Why am I reading it?"

"On the beach last night. Remember when Pat went up to Martin Ross' house?"

"Right."

"Apparently he has a desk in the living room."

"Okay."

"Pat walked past it on her way to the john and saw that note."

"And picked it up?"

"And copied it. Thought it might be important."

Barrett read it again, mumbling through it. "'Martin—guru says OK!—CC.'"

"We thought the 'CC' might stand for 'Carl Conley.' Or 'Carole.' What do *you* think?"

Barrett shrugged. "I dunno. Might stand for Charlie Chaplin for all *I* know at this point.'"

He reached for his coffee cup. The phone shrilled again, once. The answering machine whirred back into action. Barrett swallowed some coffee.

"So. You and Mrs. Pratt *both* had something you didn't tell me about last night, right?"

Sitting back in his chair, Tony nodded. "Right," he said.

The police officer sipped a little more coffee before he said, "I'm gonna say again what I said before, Mr. Pratt, and this *is* important: Don't try to do police work. That's *my* job. Stay out of it."

Tony sat up quickly and Barrett raised his hand, palm out. "Easy, Mr. Pratt!" He leaned back in his own chair, belt and holster creaking. He went on, calmly. "You and Mrs. Pratt look like nice folks. Mrs. Pratt, she seems like a real nice lady."

His eyes narrowed as he smiled across the white

rim of the cup. "Even if you *did* stick her with a pretty funny name."

Tony's return smile was tight and brief. "We haven't heard a new comment about 'Pat Pratt' since the second week of our marriage. It doesn't bother us much."

Barrett nodded and his smile went away slowly. "Yeah." He slid some papers around on his desk. "What is it again that she does?"

"She's a financial consultant."

"That's right, I remember now." Barrett tipped his coffee cup slowly back and forth. From behind another smile he said, "Not many folks can spend time at the coast on a work day. You takin' a couple of days off?—on vacation?—or what?"

Tony sat back, his left elbow resting on the desk. There was a definite edge to his voice. "We've told you all that."

The policeman leaned forward and his answer came out a little tight, too. "Mr. Pratt, a man who comes in here with evidence from the scene of a crime can't afford to get testy." He swiveled his chair and put his forearms on his desk. "Refresh my memory."

Tony's fingers drummed on the desk for a second. Then he rubbed his hands together, took a deep breath, and let his hands rest in his lap. Staring at the officer, he spoke softly. "I'm a writer. My time is pretty much my own. As for my wife, her consulting business was very active during the first six months of this year. So she's taking a few days off."

47

There was a pause before Barrett shrugged and said, questioning, "Seems to me you'd want to make sure she gets some rest—stay out of trouble—not get any more involved in this business than you have to. Why *are* you messing around in it?"

Tony shifted on the chair. "I've thought about that. One reason, I think, is this: As a writer, I'm curious about it. I've written a few mystery stories, but this is the first 'real' one I've seen and I want to follow through to find out what happens."

He leaned forward, elbows on the desk, still speaking quietly. "Another reason could be that I want to prove that we had nothing to do with this whole thing, except for finding the body—especially if it turns out to be murder."

Barrett grunted and shook his head sharply.

Tony sat up. "Another reason, just a feeling I have, is that I know what it is that I found." He looked at the metal piece on the desk. "I just can't put a name to it, yet. Maybe that's *why* I kept it. I've seen it before, or something very much like it."

"Yeah? Where."

"I don't know. That's just it. I guess I thought that, if I held onto it for a while, it would come back to me."

"And it didn't."

"No. Not yet. So I decided I'd better turn it over to you before I leave town."

Barrett, studying the metal piece, muttered to himself. "Really odd-lookin' thing. Don't think I ever . . ." Suddenly his black brows rose and his voice

48

toughened again. "Leave town? What brought that on?"

"Nothing 'brought it on.' It's a business trip to Los Angeles—been in the works for weeks. Look." Tony pulled out his wallet and showed Barrett an airline ticket folder. "The reservations were made two weeks ago."

Barrett took the ticket and checked the reservation date, the departure date, and the to/from destinations. "The ticket says 'Burbank.'" He peered at Tony. "I thought you said L.A."

"Well, you know how it is down there—a bunch of little towns stuck together to make one great big one called Los Angeles. And 'L.A.' is just sort of shorthand for the whole area. Fact is, I'm really going to Hollywood. And Studio City."

A frown began between Barrett's eyes.

Tony asked him, "Ever been to L.A.?"

Barrett returned the ticket folder and nodded, once. "Once," he said flatly, as if pronouncing sentence, and then his voice began to rise. "Took the kids to Disneyland. Got on a freeway in a string of cars maybe twenty miles long, six abreast, *just one way,* doin' 65-70 miles an hour and no more'n two feet from bumper to bumper!" He stopped and shook his head. "That's enough Mickey Mouse for me."

Tony tucked his wallet away. "I know the feeling."

Barrett shook his head again, then picked up the metal piece and studied its odd, angled grooves. Almost absently he asked Tony, "What're you doin' down there?"

"Producing some radio and TV commercials."

Barrett looked at him sharply. "You told me you're a writer."

"True. But I used to work in advertising, making commercials. Now, every once in a while the agency calls and asks me to work on a campaign, to write and produce some radio spots, shoot film or videotape, record sound tracks. That sort of thing."

There was a pause before Barrett said, "That's funny."

"What's funny?" Tony asked, expecting some kind of advertising put-down.

"There's a guy in town that does the same sort o' thing."

"Oh." Tony relaxed. "Yeah. Several people in Portland do that kind of work."

"Not Portland. I mean *here* in town."

"Musket Beach?"

"Right. Sometimes he goes to L.A. and sometimes to Portland, but sometimes he works right here. Been here four, maybe five years. Got his own recording studio and everything. Pretty fancy setup, I understand."

"Huh," Tony grunted. "What's his name?"

"Taylor. Paul Taylor. Know 'im?"

Tony nodded. "Paul Taylor? Sure. I mean, I know the name—one of the busiest actors in Hollywood. Great voice. Does voices for animated films and commercials. Radio spots, too." He paused and grunted again. "Huh. I thought he lived in L.A." Looking at Barrett he said, "So he works out of Musket Beach."

"Sure does." Suddenly, Barrett frowned and said, almost under his breath, "In more ways than one."

"What do you mean by that?"

"The hottest gossip in town is the way Mr. Taylor's been playin' around with our late mayor's wife." He glanced at Tony. "With CarolMae." Barrett tossed the metal piece onto the mess on his desk and stood up. "All that aside, Mr. Pratt, since you and Mr. Taylor are in the same line of advertising work, maybe the two of you oughta get acquainted."

"Maybe we will," Tony said, standing and pushing the chair back.

"Maybe you could do some recording together."

"Maybe we could. Speaking of working together, there's something I'd like to know."

"What's that?"

"Well, last night Martin Ross said, and it was really more like a question, that a car came tearing up his road and onto the highway just seconds before *you* came by. He was sure you saw it. And he wondered why you didn't take off after it." Tony paused. "But you didn't answer him."

Barrett reached down and with the middle finger of his left hand pushed a button on his answering machine. Over the tinny squeal of the rewinding tape he said, "Mr. Pratt, you have a nice day."

SEVEN

Wednesday Afternoon—
The Cabin

PAT sounded surprised. "And that's all he would say about it?"

Sitting on the flat top railing around the deck, she spoke to Tony while she scanned the ocean through her binoculars, watching the smooth area just beyond the breakers. The bright blue sky made the sea a matching blue and almost washed away the horizon line.

Tony leaned against the doorjamb, behind Pat and to her left, as he talked about his meeting with Barrett.

She turned to give him a quick look, irritated by what she was hearing, her voice rising as she asked, "He wouldn't tell you why he didn't go after that car? He just ignored it?"

"That's all he said. Except that I'm to be sure to call

him when I get back from Los Angeles. *And,* and I quote, 'Remember what I told you about holding things back.' Unquote."

Pat's comment was almost a sneer. "*He* should talk about holding things back!" She paused and raised her binoculars again, talking as she studied the sea and the air just above it. "Do you think that he recognized the car? That he knows who was driving it?"

Then she stopped her scan and held the glasses on one patch of water and said quietly, "Actually, *I* should talk about holding things back. I should have said something to you *and* to Barrett about that note."

Tony shrugged. "It's over. Don't worry about it."

Her binoculars still looked out to sea, but Pat looked at Tony. "By the way, wasn't he just a little bit testy about you leaving town? And speaking of that—"

Tony interrupted. "Have you seen anything out there?"

She glanced at him, then turned back to peer through the glasses. "Some brown pelicans. A long line of murres. A few cormorants. Gulls, of course, there are never no gulls. And, I think, a Caspian tern . . ."

"Good," Tony smiled.

". . . but I want to look him up in the bird book." She lowered the glasses and let them hang from the narrow black strap tucked under the collar of her camel-colored corduroy shirt. "*After* we talk about you skipping town. Again."

"Who's skipping town? It's a business trip!"

"Same thing." She swung around on the railing to face him. "Tell me something." Her hands were on her knees. "When you sold your share of the agency, I thought that you'd be out of it. Through. Finished. And I'm sure that you thought the same thing. In fact, that's why you sold it, right?—to be done with it?"

His eyebrows jumped up and his head cocked quickly to one side, agreeing. "True."

"Well, I'm just really surprised at how often they call for you to come and help. Don't those people know what they're doing?"

"Look, after all those years around the business, you know how goosey some of these advertising people get. You know how they're always asking for one more opinion, looking for another piece of research, *any*thing to make them feel a little more secure, a little more sure that they've got a campaign that's on the right track."

She tilted her head, looking at him, squinting a little. "Was it that way when you were there?"

"I prefer to think that it wasn't, but—" he smiled a little and shrugged a shoulder—"sometimes, probably, yes. But remember that they're working with ideas, mostly. Feelings. Emotions. Not facts."

She shook her head. "A funny business. I'm glad that I deal with numbers. Numbers are very unemotional."

"Well, I guess every business is strange, once in a while."

"Not many are so strange that they have to work through the Fourth of July!"

Tony shrugged. "They've got a deadline to meet."

Pat let herself slide to the deck, then she stood and leaned back against the railing, arms folded. A touch of sarcasm came into her voice. "Did you ever think that maybe those 'emotional' advertising geniuses do that on purpose? That they *let* those deadlines creep up? So all of a sudden they have to work like crazy! Eighteen- and twenty-four-hour days! Weekends! Holidays! *Now* they can feel like people who're doing something *important!*"

Tony laughed, nodding. "Could be."

"Funny business," Pat said again. She turned toward the ocean, raising her binoculars and starting another scan. "Anyway. Tell me your schedule, one more time. You'll be back Saturday?"

"Yes. Leave Portland at noon tomorrow, the third. Get into Burbank around two-thirty. To the Sheraton-Universal hotel for a meeting at about three..."

"The Sheraton-Universal? You've never stayed there before. Where is it?"

"Just a hoot 'n' a holler from Hollywood." He moved to her side and looked in the direction her binoculars were aimed. "Are you seeing anything?"

"No, want a look?" She looped the strap over her head and gave the glasses to Tony. "What's the rest of your schedule?"

He held the binoculars up to his eyes for a second and quickly snatched them away, blinking. Shaking his head, he refocused the glasses. "We've *got* to do something about your eyes."

"They work fine for me. Go ahead, you're at the hotel for a three o'clock meeting..."

"We'll work at the hotel the rest of Thursday afternoon." Tony trained the glasses on an area just beyond the breakers. "Thursday evening there's a recording session for music tracks. Friday morning, a session for voice tracks. Friday afternoon, we put the tracks and pictures together. Saturday, I leave Burbank on a three o'clock flight, get into Portland about five-thirty, and get back here to the beach in time to take you to dinner at, oh, say eight o'clock."

"Sounds very well planned, very well organized," Pat said. "But from past experience, I'd say that those well-laid plans work out about—what—two times out of five?"

He laughed and stood the glasses on the rail. "About one in five."

"I hope this is the one. I don't like to spend too much time here alone." She moved toward him. "Being by myself for a while is all right. I enjoy that." Her voice was soft and quiet now. "But sometimes at night this cabin is the only place around here with lights on; there's nobody else on this road. And if you're gone more than a couple of days I begin to feel a little spooked, a little tense."

He wrapped his arms around her shoulders. "Well, it'll only *be* for a couple of days, but if you want to go home to Portland we'll go." Shaking her head no, she put her arms around his waist. "And anyway," he went on, "you'll have lots of company this week with all the tourists in town for Sand Castle Time. And Saturday you can walk up the beach and join the crowd at the contest."

"Not me," Pat wagged her head under his chin, "I wouldn't be caught dead in that mob."

EIGHT

Thursday Afternoon—
Hollywood

In the back seat of the cab, Tony leaned forward to crank the window half-way down, compromising with the smog along the Hollywood Freeway: He wanted to feel the cool rush of air, but he was wary of air he could taste.

As always, it was a minor shock to come from Oregon's clean breezes, fir trees, pines, alders, and sensible rain parkas into the smokey sunlight, dusty palm trees, and unusual native costumes of Southern California.

And already he missed Pat. He realized that, off and on, he had been recalling bits and pieces of their most recent conversations.

She had offered to drive from Musket Beach to the Portland airport with him but he had said no, thanks, that's why we have both cars here.

Which had reminded *her* that, with both kids in college—Jenny at the University of Oregon and Dan at Oregon State—it might be time to trade the station wagon for a smaller car. He'd said that they'd probably need the wagon more than ever, now, to haul school gear back and forth.

Which had reminded *him*, when he stopped at their suburban home in Lakewood for his suitcase and raincoat, to see the kids on their first full-time summer jobs—Jenny at the Lakewood library and Dan at Burger King.

Which had reminded *both* Tony and Pat that they hadn't talked much about Jenny and Dan for the last couple of days.

And they knew the reason: The body on the beach. That grim subject had taken over most of their thoughts and much of their energy.

Because they were both caught up in the mystery, and because they had an almost proprietary feeling about "their" stretch of beach, they felt impelled to look for answers to a lot of questions.

How did Carl Conley die? Was he murdered? Or was it an accident? If he was murdered, why? And who did it? Did the same person (persons?) put the body on the beach?

And when? That short-sleeved shirt wasn't night-time beachwear; did he die in the warm afternoon sun and then wait to be dumped on the cold, dark sand? Why?

And why that particular piece of beach?—any significance? And was there any significance in that little piece of metal, whatever it was?

What about the note Pat had seen? Did it connect Martin Ross with dead Carl Conley? Or with Conley's wife, Carole? Or both? And the car that raced up Ross road and sped away—any connection?

Pat, smart lady, had some good questions about that car: Did Officer Barrett recognize it? Is that why he didn't go after it? Because he knew where it was going? And who was driving it?

And did Barrett stay behind to make sure it wasn t followed?

Tony thought back to his short phone talk with Barrett this morning, just before leaving Musket Beach.

"Musket Beach Police—Officer Barrett speaking.'

"Officer Barrett, this is Tony Pratt."

"Who? Oh, yes, Mr. Pratt. Thought you were outta town."

"Leaving in a few minutes. Just wanted to ask about the medical examiner's report on the mayor's . . ."

"Not in yet, Mr. Pratt."

". . . and whether you've had any further thoughts about the car that was . . ."

"Not a one."

"Well, just thought I'd ask."

"Right. Mr. Pratt?"

"Yes?"

"You've heard the saying 'curiosity killed the cat?'"

"Sure."

"Well, *some* people say that's wrong."

"Oh? What do *they* say killed the cat?"

"Got run over by a car."

And Barrett hung up.

The cab stopped, snapping Tony from yesterday in Oregon to here and now in Southern California.

For a second he thought the car was stalled in the middle of the Hollywood Freeway, but then he realized that he must have been daydreaming when the driver took the freeway exit, because now they were waiting for the traffic light at Cahuenga and Lankershim. They made the turn onto Lankershim, then another quick turn, and swung up the long driveway to the hotel entrance.

"Wait a minute," Tony muttered to himself, getting out of the cab. "Lankershim?"

He plopped his bag and briefcase down on the hot, gray concrete sidewalk and slung his raincoat over his shoulder. Bending down, he leaned into the opened rear doorway. He handed a bill to the driver, whose blond hair and beard were far too gray for the lavender caftan and puka shell beads he was wearing. Tony could almost see a peace sign painted on his forehead.

The driver was turned part-way around on the

front seat. He nodded at Tony's raincoat. "You expecting rain, man?"

"Someday," Tony said. "Listen, didn't we pass Lankershim out there by the airport, on the way to the freeway?"

"Right," the driver said, counting Tony's change across the seatback.

"Then why didn't we take Lankershim instead of the freeway? It comes right here to the hotel."

The driver's pale, bony hand came back over the seat and plucked the tip Tony held out. "Man, I didn't pack enough lunch for a trip like that."

"Slow, huh?"

The pale hand closed around the tip and made a fist, thumb straight out. The driver squinted at Tony along the thumb. "Would I lie to a man who comes to L.A. with a raincoat? In July?"

NINE

Thursday Afternoon—Hollywood (continued)

"WE'RE in Bonham's room, suite—802. Save me A.A."

Tony dialed suite 802, looking at the note again, admiring the thick, black, calligraphic strokes of Abe Arthur's writing. "Abe must be the only art director in California still using a real pen with real ink," he said to himself.

He dropped his room key on the bedside table and stretched out on the tan quilted bedspread, the phone balanced on his belly. In the middle of the fifth ring a deep, slightly nasal voice answered. "Bonham residence, Abe The Maid speaking."

"Good afternoon, Abe The Maid, this is Mr. Pratt."

"Ah, Mr. Pratt. You got my message?"

"Yes, but I thought I should call before coming 'round, in the event that you and the group had, perhaps, adjourned for a swim."

"No, sir! Too busy for *that*, Mr. Pratt. And may I suggest, sir, that you get your ass in here?"

"Yes, ma'am."

Tony opened the door to Gary Bonham's suite and out rolled a cloud of blue-gray smoke. Mixed with the stinking, closed-room smell of dead cigarettes came the familiar bitter bite of Abe Arthur's cigar and the sweet flowery dance of Ken Reedy's Dunhill pipe tobacco.

Leaving the door open, Tony walked in, squinting through the smoke. Abe twisted around. Cigar ashes sprayed across his blue button-down shirt, but his gray eyes were grinning behind his black horn-rimmed glasses. Reedy sat still, hunched over the bowl of a huge meerschaum pipe almost as large as his nose, his narrow hooded eyes scanning the other people in the room, alert for cues.

Abe and Reedy sat in low white wicker chairs on one side of a wicker-based, glass-topped coffee table piled high with advertising layouts, full-page and double-truck ads that vibrated with cheery, comic-page colors.

Across the table from Abe and Reedy, Gary Bonham roosted on the edge of a pastel-flowered couch. Marion Wallingford, The Client, cuddled in a corner of the couch with a Bloody Mary.

Tony crossed the room and said loudly, "Somebody in here is a heavy smoker!"

Looking up at Tony, Bonham ground another half-smoked Marlboro into a heaped ashtray. "Must be Reedy and his stinking pipe," he said smoothly.

"Right," Abe growled. "They're both overweight. Throw 'em out. But save his nose. We'll use it for a sunshade by the pool."

Reedy's hands shot up and formed a tent sheltering his nose. "Jeez," he whined, "with friends like these . . ."

"Who needs enemas, right?" Abe asked.

"Hi, Gary," Tony said to Bonham.

"Glad you could make it, Tony." Flashing his Essence-of-Ad-Man smile, Bonham bounced up from the sofa. Tall, gray at the short-trimmed temples, trim as a ferret and tweedy as any Brooks Brother, Gary Bonham was Managing Director in the San Francisco office of Farnham, Andersen, Ryan, & Taylor Advertising, the big Chicago-based agency that had bought Tony's agency three years before, primarily to take over the Well-Fed Baking Company account.

Bonham was the only man in the stuffy room wearing a suit. He shook Tony's hand with a supermanly grip, nodding toward the couch and the small figure nestling in the cushions, nearly lost among the lavender pansies. "You know The Client, of course."

Marion Wallingford, Director of Advertising for Well-Fed Bread, clutched his Bloody Mary glass with both hands. A wildly-flowered shirt almost fell off his narrow little shoulders; his too-thin neck carefully balanced his too-big head; aviator style glasses slipped down his beaky nose. The filter tip of a Benson & Hedges smoldered in a volcano-shaped mound of cigarette butts in the ashtray beside him on the cushions.

"Of course. Marion, how are you? And how are things in Minneapolis?"

The delicately manicured fingers of Wallingford's right hand uncurled from around his drink and swam in the air. He bared his broad, moose-like teeth. "I'll be better when we've solved the problems some of your friends have got us into." Under half-closed lids, his bloodshot little eyes picked at the other people in the room as his hand slid out of Tony's and curled around his glass again.

Shoving another wicker chair up to the low table with the layouts, Tony smiled and said, "There *are* no problems, Marion, only opportunities."

"Jeee-*zus*," Abe Arthur growled.

Tony sat down beside him, winked, and pulled a pad of yellow paper and a ballpoint pen from his briefcase.

Bonham walked around the end of the couch and stood behind it, apparently ready to make a speech. "Tony, we're in a box and we've got to get out or we're in deep in the proverbial creek." He leaned forward, hands flared on the back of the flowered cushions. "Now let me paint in broad strokes . . ."

"Hold it!" Marion Wallingford squealed and shifted on the sofa, holding up his glass. "Reedy, fix me a drink!"

"Sure thing, Boss!" Reedy sprang from his chair,

snatched the empty glass, and scurried to the tan wicker bar in the corner.

Tony looked at Abe, who looked back. Through hard experience, they knew that Ken Reedy had his shortcomings as a copywriter, including an inability to write two consecutive complete sentences on one subject. "But he gets good drinks," Abe muttered. "And if you watch closely, you can see his tail wag."

"Marion," Gary Bonham said, mildly protesting his client's interruption. "I'm just trying to put Tony into the picture!"

Wallingford pushed himself away from the pillows and wailed, "We're *all* up to our *ass* in the picture, Gary!" He sat back, tucking his legs under him and wriggling into the sofa's corner. "Now we have to solve what you perceive as a *problem* in the picture."

Reedy held a fresh drink in front of Wallingford and he took it without even a glance of thanks. Continuing in an irritated, we've-been-through-all-this-before tone, he said, "We're all in agreement that we've got a sound concept for marketing bread: A cartoon-type, Pied Piper-type character leading a bunch of kids through an imaginery place called Sandwich Town . . ."

"Well-Fed *Bread* Sandwich Town," Reedy put in.

The middle finger on Wallingford's right hand uncurled from his glass, stiffened, pointed at Reedy, and curled around his glass again. "And we've got great radio spots. Great TV spots. Great four-color ads for the

Sunday comics. All kinds of entertaining, fun stuff. Very appealing, very warm, very friendly and—"

"There!" Bonham firmly interrupted his client. "That's my point!" He hurried around to the front of the couch.

"Tony! Look!" he said eagerly, eyes excited, face red under his California tan. Squatting on the edge of the couch by the coffee table, he pointed at the top layout. "Tell me what you see in that layout!"

Tony glanced at the familiar drawing and said calmly, "Just what Marion says: A kid's cartoon village— little kids on bikes, swings, slides . . ."

Bonham shouted impatiently. "Animals! Any animals?" He leaned so far forward that he almost slid off the couch.

"Sure," Tony said, pointing. "A couple of dogs, a cat, a deer, a little dragon—"

"That's it!" Bonham smashed his fist down on the layout. "That's it!" he yelled again. He jumped up, towering over the coffee table, triumphant. Pointing a shaking finger at the simple, child-like drawing he bellowed, "What's that son-of-a-bitchin' *dragon* doing in *Sandwich Town!*"

As Bonham stood there in the ringing silence, a Lancelot in natural-shoulder armor, Tony looked at the others.

Abe's face was a stone mask, but his laughing eyes were beginning to flood.

Wallingford drunk, almost lapped, from his glass. Reedy sucked blue puffs out of his pipe, his eager

70

little eyes shining like a dog's, searching every face for his cue.

Tony wiped a hand across his mouth. He spoke quietly, soothingly emphasizing key words. "Gary. These are *ads*. They're *cartoons*. For the *funny papers*."

Bonham, standing tall, waggled his finger at the ad. "That's not the point! The point is: All the *other* animals in Sandwich Town are *real*." He sat on the edge of the couch again and explained, taking Tony into his confidence, trying to make him understand something that all the others had missed. "But *dragons* aren't real. They're *mythical* creatures!"

Abe squinted at Bonham over his black frames. He sat back. In the solemn silence, his wicker chair creaked. It creaked again as he crossed his legs and shoved his right hand into his pants pocket and jingled the coins there.

Tony glanced quickly at Abe. He seemed to know, when he heard the chinking coins, that Abe had made a decision.

To Bonham, Tony said, "So what you're saying, Gary, is that the ads would be okay without the dragon."

"Right." Bonham smiled. "Exactly!" And he opened his arms wide in a gesture that said to the others, "You see? I told you that Tony would understand."

Tony turned to Abe, who nodded, then turned to Wallingford, who shrugged.

Reedy, spotting the nod and the shrug, leaped to his feet, stabbed the stem of his pipe at Abe and ordered, "Kill the dragon!"

71

But Abe had already humped his chair forward. Leaning over the layout, he pulled out one of his Eagle drafting pencils.

"What do you think?" Tony asked him.

Abe craned his head around and squinted at Tony through a puff of cigar smoke. "We shall replace the mythic dragon."

He drew a few quick lines on the layout and sat back. Head cocked to the right, eyes squinting, he peered at the drawing. Then he spun it around for Bonham to look at and grinned a wide, innocent grin behind his cigar. "Whaddaya say, Gary?"

Bonham looked at the drawing and then raised his arms in smiling surrender. "Perfect." He almost crooned. "A unicorn!"

TEN

Thursday Afternoon— Musket Beach

Pat's meander among the tables at the Musket Beach Book Store stopped abruptly when she heard the word. It was the same unusual word that had caught her eye when she walked through Martin Ross' house and saw the telephone message on his desk. But here in the bookstore, it jumped at her out of another customer's conversation. Accented by a high-pitched giggle, it came in the middle of a gossipy sentence: "... and some *guru* wants to buy the whole thing! That's what *I* heard."

Casually, Pat looked around the small shop. A thin, tan woman with weathered blonde hair leaned a dungareed hip against the counter by the cash register while she nattered at the bookstore owner. Above the prissy sounds of Vivaldi from the stereo speakers, over the constant jumble of talking, laughing, shuffling tourists, and despite the occasional honk and hum of Main Street traffic heard through the open door, the word flew across the small shop and pinned Pat where she stood.

"... some *guru* wants to buy the whole thing!"

At a tiny desk behind the counter, the little round owner raised her wide round face and frowned. The corners of her mouth turned down and she shook her frizzed red hair. In a flat monotone she said to the blonde, "That's all we need in this town, a few more flakes."

The blonde's loud explosive "Ha!" turned a few heads her way for a moment, but the bookstore owner went on. "Who's handling the deal? Somebody from Portland? Or a local realtor?" She pronounced it "reel-a-tor."

Pat, without looking up, began making her way slowly toward the conversation. The few other customers—tourists, apparently in town for the weekend, uninterested in local affairs—resumed their unheeding shuffle through the shop. Pat found two books she'd been looking for, picked them up, and ambled even closer to the counter.

Answering the owner's question, the blonde shook her head, swinging her hair along the shoulders of her fishnet sweater. "I don't know who's got the deal. Haven't heard. The only thing I know for sure is: Carl Conley won't be handling it!"

The owner's eyes looked up at the blonde. Smirking, she said, "When was the last time Carl Conley handled *any*thing! Including that so-called 'wife' of his!"

At this, the blonde stiffened her bony shoulders and took a deep breath, apparently ready to launch into a long speech, but the owner cut it off before it got started. She held up a cautioning hand and ducked her head a bit. "I know, I know," she said quickly. "'Don't speak ill of the dead' and all that. But I'm not saying anything to you that I didn't say to Carl Conley. Right to his face."

The shop owner got up from her desk and leaned over the counter toward her friend. She spoke quietly, but she was so intense that her voice carried to Pat, crossing in front of the open door.

"The stupid bastard took Verna's nice real estate business and turned it belly up. From the day she married him till the day she died, he never sold doodley-squat!" With a scornful gesture she tossed her receipt book down on her desk. "Then he takes the money Verna left and starts chasin' that Little Miss Hot-Buns or whatever her name is and spends the *rest* of Verna's money—jewelry, clothes. Jeez. Young enough to be his daughter, for chrissakes, and he marries her and takes her to *Disneyland* on a for-chrissakes *honeymoon!* Can you *believe* it?"

The blonde customer shook her head, saying, "Calm down, now, Maggie."

"Rita, you shouldn't have got me started on Carl Conley. 'Mayor' Carl Conley," she added. "Jeez." She raked her bony fingers through her hair. "I'm not the

75

only one around here who feels this way. A lot of other people in this town have the same opinion of Carl Conley." She jabbed an index finger at the blonde. "And you know it, too. The only reason we voted for him was to make Verna feel good. So what happens? Verna dies and he marries Miss Two-Boobs. And apparently he couldn't do doodley with her, either, the way she runs around with that freaky little actor. Now Conley's got himself killed, the poor bastard, and nobody knows who, what, when, where, or why."

Her angry eyes were still focused on Carl Conley when she turned to Pat and said, "Poor, stupid bastard!"

Then she caught herself and her right hand flew up and covered her mouth as her left reached out to Pat in a softening gesture. "Oh, I'm sorry," she apologized with a laugh, "I didn't mean you."

Pat nodded and gave a little smile and said, "I know—I couldn't help hearing part of what you said." She pushed her two new M.K. Wren mystery novels across the counter. "So, I understand." Then she looked at the blonde and back to the shop owner, pausing before she said, "My husband and I are the ones who found Carl Conley's body."

The blonde gasped and her left hand went quickly to her cheek, then she twisted her wrist and a finger pointed at Pat just as the shop owner said, "Then you must be Mrs. Platt."

"*Pratt*," came a man's correcting voice, over Pat's shoulder. "This here's Miz *Pratt*."

Pat whirled around as the bookstore owner said,

"Why, Martin Ross, what brings you in here?—makin' the Christmas collection already?"

"No, I just seen Miz Pratt, through the window," Ross said quietly. He reached around Pat and picked up one of her new books before saying, with a soft smile, "And I thought it might be interesting to see what she reads in her *own* house."

Turning back to the counter to pay for the books, Pat froze. Slowly, she looked again at Martin Ross, first at his friendly round face, then at his cold, hard, hooded eyes staring into hers.

Without even glancing at the book, he handed it back to Pat. Taking it, she felt the same quick quiver through her fingers and all through her body—the same feeling she'd had when she came back from Ross' house and stood on the bank above the beach, staring down at him staring up at her.

Now, standing by the counter and looking at each other again, Pat nodded as if he'd whispered, "I know what you saw on my desk. And now you *know* that I know."

Surprised into silence by her feelings, Pat turned away and paid for her books without a word. As the owner fumbled under the counter for a paper bag, noise and commotion began tumbling in from outside. Through the open door came a loud babble of voices with an odd, questioning quality about it. Then the voices mingled with a clinking, ringing chime and with a rhythmic fluttering of drums rising and falling in the high, flat tones of bongos or timbales.

77

"What in tarnation . . ." Martin Ross muttered, bustling out through the door ahead of the blonde. Pat and four or five other customers hurried out followed by the store owner, after she slid Pat's books into a small sack and dropped it on the counter as she scooted around it. Outside, they all bunched together on the narrow wooden front porch above the sidewalk and echoed the questions running through the crowd on the street.

"What's happening?" the blonde asked, of nobody in particular and everybody in general. The only answer she got—and unsatisfactory, at that—came from the store owner, who hopped up on the wooden bench in front of the store windows and croaked, "What the hell's going on!"

Boosting herself up on the bench beside the owner, Pat joined the chorus. "What is it?" she asked, looking to her right down Main Street. "Can you see anything?"

"Some kind of a parade, looks like. All dressed in blue."

"Who are they? A local club?"

The drums were getting louder. The people around her answered with shrugs and headshakes. No one on the porch seemed to know anything about the parade until suddenly the blonde yelled, "The Faithful Ones!"

"What?"

"It's a commune or a sect or something." The drumming was closer and louder, but she shouted over the clatter. "'The Faithful Ones.' I heard about 'em a few months ago in Idaho. They got kicked out of California so they moved to Boise, and then they got kicked out of Boise, so . . ."

"So they're coming here?"

"Right. 'Let's try Ory-gawn.' That's what their guru said."

"*Guru?*" Martin Ross stood very still for a moment, before he turned and shouted at the blonde, "What do you know about the guru?"

The noise was so intense that the blonde's answer was a wide-eyed shake of her head. Ross peered at her for another second, then turned away.

People were lining both sides of Main Street now, and looking south toward Woody's Goody Shoppe and the bank. Some had edged into the two-lane street between parked cars, standing on tiptoes and craning their necks for a better view.

In the northbound lane, cars moved ahead as fast as they could go without running over people. But in the southbound lane, traffic had stopped dead. Frowning, frustrated drivers pounded on their steering wheels, blasted their horns in maddening staccato bursts, and twisted their heads around looking for a way out of the jam.

Pat turned and looked north, to her left. At the corner, half a block away—the corner with the stop sign, where the road from Highway 101 came into town—Officer Barrett stood in the intersection frantically directing traffic. Stopping the incoming southbound cars, he waved them off of Main Street. At the same time he tried to speed the northbound cars out of town or onto a side street.

As Pat watched, a rusty Chevy pickup truck wheeled across the intersection and bounced up onto the sidewalk not far from Barrett. The driver parked on the sidewalk in front of the hardware store and hopped down. Running into the street, he pulled on the red jacket that showed he was a Musket Beach Volunteer Fireman. When he reached Barrett, the fireman and the cop stood nose-to-nose amid the uproar and yelled and waved at each other for a few seconds, then the fireman took Barrett's place in the intersection and the officer turned and walked down the middle of Main Street toward Pat, toward the oncoming parade, and into the traffic jam that had become a madhouse. Horns blew, turn signals flashed, motors raced, exhaust smoke and smells smothered everything, and through it all—rhythmic, throbbing, insistent—came the ringing beat of drums and tambourines.

As the north lane cleared, some of the southbound cars made tight, tire-squealing U-turns and drove off. A couple of others pulled into the parking lot between Martin Ross' grocery store and the bakery. Others, driving too close together or not reacting fast enough, were caught in a flood of human flesh.

The parade was a moving wall of people, ten and twelve abreast, row after row after row, from sidewalk to sidewalk. The tourists and locals who'd been strolling

along, enjoying their weekend at the beach or doing
their shopping, were suddenly stopped in their tracks,
pressed back against the walls and storefronts or forced
to run ahead of the pack, darting and dodging around
the cars trying to get off the street. And the cars that
didn't get away were swamped and overrun, the people
trapped inside.

Pat looked at Barrett, now standing in the street in
front of the bookstore, a lone police officer caught in
the middle of a human maelstrom, helpless. Pat could
see it. Barrett saw it, too. He began shoving his way
through the crowd toward the sidewalk, glancing from
face to face, nodding when he saw Martin Ross, nodding
again when he caught sight of Pat.

By the time he got to the sidewalk in front of the
bookstore, at least twenty ranks of paraders had passed
by, all dressed in blue—baby-blue robes, baby-blue
tunics, baby-blue pants. They were men and women, tall
and short, thin and fat, bearded and smooth, bald and
hairy. They were either tanned or sunburned.

The drumming was louder than ever, but every
face in the parade smiled calmly, as though its owner
had just remembered something quite pleasant. Each
pair of eyes roamed over the watching and partially
hostile crowd, showing no interest at all in what they
were seeing.

From her perch on the bench, Pat watched Barrett
push his way across the sidewalk and up the bookstore's
two front steps, squeezing into the crowd on the narrow

81

porch. When he turned around to view the marchers over the heads of the people on the sidewalk, he was standing next to Martin Ross and in front of Pat.

Ross, grim and angry, yelled at Barrett, "Wonderful people you sign parade permits for!"

"They got no permit. They just *did* it."

"But why?" Pat asked. "What's the point?"

"Maybe to put on a show," Barrett answered. "And maybe to show how many there are." He looked at Ross. "Anyway, Martin, I thought they were *your* friends."

Glancing back at Pat, Ross shook his head. "I got no friends that'd tear up *my* town like this! Why don't you stop 'em?"

Barrett's head reared back. "Ha!" He motioned at the rows and rows of people marching past in a blue stream. "Be my guest!" He looked down the street and then turned back to Ross. "Start with him!" he yelled, jabbing his thumb to his right. "Try a citizen's arrest on *that* guy."

Pat looked out, in the direction Barrett had pointed. There was a break in the parading blue ranks approaching the front of the bookstore. In the center of the open space a long, shiny, baby-blue Rolls Royce moved majestically down the center of Main Street. Standing in the Rolls, in what appeared to be a Plexiglas bubble, a tall, thin, blonde-bearded man bowed and waved, bowed and waved, turned to the other side and bowed and waved. His bare bald head gleamed in the sunlight, matching the brilliant reflections flashing from his long gold robe.

As Pat watched the Rolls Royce pass in front of the bookstore, the man standing in the car, bowing and waving, looked in her direction. For just a fraction of a second—almost like a freeze-frame shot in a movie— his eyes found and focused on someone on the porch with Pat, and at the edge of her vision she saw both Ross and Barrett stiffen, apparently in recognition.

Men in blue tunics and blue pants surrounded the car, two in front, one at each fender and each door, two behind. But these men seemed different from the others in the parade. There was a difference in their appearance, in the way they moved, in their attitude of vigilance. Each wore sunglasses, each carried a walkie-talkie radio, and each kept his head moving constantly, watching the crowd, the buildings, everything along the street.

Directly behind the Rolls Royce came two Jeep C-Js, side by side, carrying four more men apiece, men who acted exactly like those guarding the Rolls. In both Jeeps two of the men stood, hands on the roll bar, looking the crowd over. Every few seconds, the man on the right spoke a few words into his radio microphone.

From somewhere, possibly a tape machine and loudspeaker in one of the Jeeps, a woman's warm, deep voice said over and over: "The Loved One extends his love and his blessing. May your day be filled with love. The Loved One extends his love and his blessing. May your day be filled with love. The Loved One extends . . ."

Musket Beach had never seen anything quite like

it. Tourists and locals along the sidewalks stood and stared—at the Rolls Royce and the Jeeps, at The Loved One and his guardians—as if they were watching props and actors in a play that no one understood.

As the main part of the parade passed, the noise began to die. The drums and cymbals faded first, then the loudspeaker. Finally, there was just the scuff of sandals on the street as a few more rows of blue-clad marchers shuffled past the bookstore, looking warily at the drivers along the curbs and in the parking lot who began to gun engines and pull into the street.

People on the sidewalk and the porch began milling around, too, making almost as much noise as the parade, buzzing and rumbling with gossip, discussions, and arguments about the unexpected spectacle they'd just seen.

On the bookstore porch, Martin Ross and Officer Barry Barrett looked out at the end of the parade, shaking their heads. Behind them, Pat and the bookstore owner stepped down from their perch on the bench. The owner nudged Pat in the ribs and winked, pointing to Ross' back. "Well, Martin," she said loudly, "how nice of you to put on a parade for us. What a great idea for a Thursday afternoon."

Ross jumped as though she'd jabbed him with a pin. He whirled and glared at her with hard, dry eyes. "You picked the wrong man to be funny to, Maggie, and the wrong time." His voice was tight, too, the words pinched out through clenched teeth. "And I'll tell you somethin' else." He glanced at Barrett and down to Barrett's pistol

84

and back. "If I had a gun, I'd *never* let trash like that into my town." He spun around again, bumped into Barrett, and almost fell as he stumbled off the porch and stalked away toward his store.

"Well!" said Pat. "A trifle bombastic, I *must* say."

Maggie shrugged. "Martin's always been protective about this town, but I'm beginning to think he's going a little overboard." She shook her head sympathetically. "Sometimes Martin acts like he's lost a few logs off his load." Then she snapped her fingers and pointed at Pat. "Oh! Your books!" And she ran inside her store to get Pat's package.

Pat turned to Barrett. "What about the parade, or whatever it was," she said. "As far as I could see, except for the fact that those people wear funny clothes they seem to be a peaceable looking bunch."

Barrett looked at her and his eyes narrowed as he said, "They may *look* peaceable, but from what I hear, from reports I get, I'll guarantee that under those funny blue outfits there's either a .38 or a rifle."

Maggie came out and handed Pat her new books. "Have fun with the mysteries," she said.

ELEVEN

*Thursday Night—
Hollywood*

At American Recording Studios, Tony paused and looked along the narrow hallway leading to Studio A. The gray-painted walls and the polished old black linoleum floor stopped at two faraway doors. One led straight into Studio A; the other was set into the hall at a slight angle and opened into Control Room A. Above each door a small red bulb burned dully, the centers of two pale pink, overlapping haloes.

The lobby, the hallway, the whole building had an aura. There was a pulse, a beat, a feeling. It felt as though it was never left alone, as though people were always at it, always using it, always there. Night after day, day after night, endless rounds of recording sessions left small bits and pieces embedded in the walls, residues of old smoke, old coffee, old booze and breath mints, old sweat and perfume and aftershave, old breath blown through warm horns and quivering throats. All the old notes, all of their music, days and nights and years of music were still there, somehow caught and held, preserved in the countless tiny holes of the tired acoustical panels covering the walls and ceilings, caught and held, echoing softly, even as new tracks were laid over them.

Along the left wall of the hall, open instrument cases littered a long row of blue plastic-cushioned window seats. Smoke smudged up from knee-high, sand-filled ashtrays smoldering with cigar and cigarette butts.

The right wall was lined with tall coin machines, their dirty, clouded little windows hawking cigarettes, soft drinks, candy bars, chewing gum, mints, antacid tablets, apples, oranges, breakfast rolls, sandwiches, coffee, soup, hot chocolate, and change.

Above the studio doors, the red lights went off and Tony headed toward the control room door at the end of the hall. A percussion outfit, packed for transfer to another session across town, almost blocked his way: two kettle drums, marimba, bass drum, tom-toms, congas, bongos, stacked cymbals, and snare drum, all in strapped black cases with drummer Lem Richards's famous name stenciled in white.

Tony rattled his fingers against a conga drum case and reached for the handle on the air-lock door, leaning back a little to pull against its heavy resistance. It gave a sucking sound as it opened on a cubicle about three feet square, with another door on the opposite side. He stepped in and across the cubicle. The soundproof door whooshing shut behind him made his ears tingle with the pressure change. Pulling the second door open, a high-pitched screech hit him in the face.

Tony went up the four steps into the nearly dark booth. The front quarter of the booth, down and to his left, was on the same level as the studio. But the rest of the small room, the part that held all the recording equipment, was raised about three feet above the studio floor. Two sixteen-track recording machines were rewinding music tapes at top speed, gates closed. A screaming, skin-prickling gabble pounded through two thirty-inch speakers mounted on a front wall that sloped down to double-paned windows looking into the bright studio.

Inside the small room, Tony seemed to be the only person who noticed the noise. The other men in the shadowy, smokey booth seemed completely unaware of the shrill, ear-shattering noise. One, on the lower level, was even using the telephone.

The tapes, rewinding, hit silent leader almost simultaneously and the sudden quiet was nearly as shocking as the noise had been. It caught Irwin Jackson—arranger, composer, conductor—yelling into the phone: "RIGHT! NBC AT NINE!" Then, realizing that the tapes had stopped, he went "Oop!" and looked around at the machines as he went on speaking in his normal, gravelly voice. "Sorry about your ear, babes," he said into the phone. "Yeah, nine o'clock tonight, NBC. Right.

Glad you can make it, Suze. That's cool. Right. Bye, babes."

Jackson stood and reached up to put the phone back on the console table, on the platform. He looked up at Tony. His long arms spread wide and he tossed his head back in an I-give-up attitude. "Tonight!" he shouted, wagging his head. "*Jee*-zus!" The dim overhead lights danced over his thin, brown horn-rimmed glasses while the bright lights from the studio beamed a halo off his bald head. Then he relaxed, scratching at his gray-black beard.

"Video screw-up on that NBC special we just recorded," he told Tony. "Got to retape some stuff *tonight*. After *your* session! Thank God all the same singers can make it!"

He walked across the lower level at the front of the control room, past a row of six theater-type seats set up for clients and visitors. A few feet in front of the seats, huge double-glazed soundproof windows looked into the studio where the orchestra sat on metal folding chairs in a small forest of music stands and microphones.

In the control room, behind and above the row of client seats, ran a long, wide counter. Its right end held the sound-mixing console. Scattered over the rest of the counter were scripts, music scores, pens and pencils, talk-back mikes, timer-control buttons, and such other essential recording session equipment as cigarette packages, cigarette lighters, dirty ashtrays, and white Styrofoam cups half-filled with cold coffee. Behind the counter, looking out into the studio, were chairs for the director, producer, arranger, and sound mixer. In the semidark against the three remaining walls, lights glittered and glowed and winked on the various tape recording machines—a 24-track Ampex, two 16-track Ampexes, and an old two-track Sculley.

Jackson hopped up the steps of the console platform. "Well, whatever happens, happens," he said, holding his right hand out to Tony. "Good to see you, Tones."

They shook hands. "How've you been, Jax?" Tony asked as he put his briefcase on the chair at the left end of the counter.

"What can I tell you," Jackson shrugged, smiling and draping his brown leather jacket on the chair at the center of the console. "The good news is: I'm here! The bad news I haven't heard yet." He shrugged again. "So why worry."

Jackson waved a hand at the small, bald, bony man in front of the console. "You've worked with master mixer Marty Belcher, I believe."

The engineer twisted around, nodding and smiling, his hands never losing contact with the switches, dials, and buttons on his control board.

"Right, right," Jackson went on, without giving anyone a chance to do more than nod and wave. "And our tape operators are Gino and Wally." He waved an arm toward two young engineers at the tall 16-track recorders against the rear wall.

Tony nodded greetings again as Jackson rubbed his

hands together a couple of times and said, "Right, right. Now, time is money, you know, so we've already laid down a couple of music tracks. Just rehearsing. To check the mike setup. So, would you like to hear 'em, Tones? To see what you think about 'em? Tony . . . ?"

Tony had turned away from Jax. Without a word, he walked slowly toward the back of the room, toward the Sculley recorder that stood between the two 16-track machines. Light from one of the pin spots overhead fanned down and spread a dull gleam on the machine's metallic face, on its spools, spindles, and wheels.

"Tones?" Jackson followed Tony, questioning.

Tony stood over the tape machine, staring down at its top. And when he spoke, he sounded like a distant echo of Officer Barrett. "Well, I'll be damned," he said. Bolted to the housing covering the machine's recording heads was a duplicate of the metal piece he'd picked up by Carl Conley's body.

He straightened, arching his back and glaring into the overhead light as his right hand reached out and moved over the narrow channels and grooves. "I should have known," he muttered to himself. "Dammit, I should've known as soon as I saw it. An editing block!"

A little later that night, Pat stood by the hatch-cover coffee table, frowning and pressing the telephone against her right ear.

"It's a what?" she asked again. "I'm not sure this is such a good connection."

She heard Tony shift his phone and repeat "An *editing* block."

The long-distance line carried only crackles and snaps from the cabin s wood stove until Pat said, "I guess I m still not understanding.'

There was a pause before Tony s voice came slowly and clearly from his Hollywood hotel room. "You use it to edit recording tape, quarter-inch recording tape'

Pat smiled and nodded. "Oh, *edit*! E-d-i-t?"

"Right," he cheered.

She sat on the edge of the couch and her voice went a little flat as she said, "'Editing' is a funny word to hear on the phone, y'know"

"Anyway, now you understand what I'm talking about."

"Well, I've heard you *talk* about it a few times, but you ve never really explained it."

"Okay." He paused, then went on, carefully putting his words in descriptive groups. "That metal block is about five inches long, right? Flat? About half-an-inch high? Maybe an inch wide?"

Pat kept putting in, "Yes. Uh-huh. Yes. Right," and bobbing her head.

"With a groove down its long flat top, right?"

"Right. Right."

"Well," he said, "it came from the top of a tape-recording machine ..."

"Really?"

"... by the recording heads. It's usually bolted on, but sometimes it's glued on. Or taped on, with double-sided tape."

"So that's why the sticky spots on the bottom," Pat said. Then she said, "Hmm," and paused.

Tony waited a few moments before he asked, "What's the matter?"

"If it's just taped on, can't you just pull it off?"

"It has to be absolutely firm—can't slip or move even a fraction of an inch when you're cutting or splicing. So the people at the recording studio said they really glue it down. They said that you almost have to hit one of those things with a hammer to knock it off."

"Huh." There was a silence and then Pat sat back on the couch and said, "Okay. Go ahead."

"Go ahead?"

"You're going to tell me how it works, right?"

"No."

"No?" Pat sounded surprised. "Why no?"

"I only wanted to tell you that I finally found out what that piece of metal is. And where it comes from." Then he added, a little bitterly, "And that I *should* have remembered as soon as I saw it, dammit."

She commiserated with him. "No need to kick yourself around. You know what it is now."

"Anyway," his voice picked up, "that's all we really need to know: that it came off of a recording machine."

"Okay."

"Besides," he went on, with a bantering tone, "I've told you before how we edit tape."

She sat up, and there was a little suspicion in her voice when she said, "You've done what?"

"I've told you about editing tape. Just as you've

94

explained to me, several times, what it means when the Federal Reserve discount rate drops half a point?"

She leaned back and said with a smile, "I see."

"Or why we should buy municipal bonds."

Wrapping and unwrapping the phone cord around an index finger, Pat continued to smile. "Some things we want to know and some things we just take on faith, is that it?"

"Seems to be."

There was a long, communicating silence before Tony said quietly, "I miss you."

And just as quietly Pat answered, "I miss you, too."

Another silence.

Then she suddenly remembered and sat up and said excitedly, "Now let me tell you *my* news!"

Pat repeated the conversation she'd heard in the bookstore, making sure that Tony understood the store owner's sour attitude about Carl Conley, his work in real estate, and his new young wife. She was also sure to tell him that other people in Musket Beach seemed to have the same opinion.

Then she described Martin Ross' sudden appearance in the store, and his cold stare, and her feeling that "Ross knows I saw that telephone message about the guru."

Keeping her story in sequence, Pat told about seeing the guru—The Loved One—and about the near-riot of a parade staged by his followers, The Faithful Ones. She mentioned the watchful men in the Jeeps who could, she said, pass for a baby blue branch of the Secret

Service. And, almost word for word, she reported Officer Barrett's bet that the guards were carrying guns.

She also talked about the way Martin Ross had stomped off after telling Barrett that he, Ross, wouldn't let things like that go on "in *my* town, not if *I* had a gun!"

"Strange reaction."

"Strange personality," Pat said. "In fact, he comes close to being a truly significant anal pore."

There was a pause, and Tony said, "I know the type."

"And another funny thing about Martin Ross is, people always seem surprised to see him. It's as though he's very seldom out and about, never around town except when it's time to raise money for something— the Christmas decorations or the Sand Castle Contest or something. But now, this week, everywhere I go, there's Martin Ross!"

She hesitated, and then went on in a somewhat bitter tone, "I almost have the feeling he's following me."

"Really?" Tony's voice had an edge of concern. "Do you want to go on back home? To Portland?"

"No-no," came Pat's quick response. And then a short laugh. "Actually, he's beginning to make me a little mad! Besides, you'll be back soon."

"A day and a half."

"Good."

They were quiet for a moment, and he asked, "What are you thinking?"

"I was wondering."

"So, what are you wondering?"

"I was wondering: Now that you've found out about that editing doo-hickey, now that we know what we know, what do we know?"

It was Tony's turn to pause, before he said quietly, "Maybe too much."

"Maybe," Pat said. "Let's see," and her voice began to pick up as she ticked off things they'd heard or discovered. "We know that the body we found was Carl Conley's; that he had a wife, his second wife, named Carole; that a note to Martin Ross about some 'guru' was signed with the initials 'CC,' meaning maybe Carl Conley . . ."

". . . or maybe Carole . . ."

"True. That there are rumors about a big real estate deal and Conley is involved somehow; that Carole Conley is fooling around with that actor, Paul Taylor. Also true?"

"That last item may just be pointless gossip."

"Lots of people seem to be passing it around, though. So we'll see." She picked up her pace again. "We also know that the thing you found by the body is an editing block that's used in recording. We know of one person in Musket Beach who has a recording studio. So we probably know where the thing came from. So we *may* know who dropped it on the beach." Her voice dropped and slowed as she stared, eyes wide, across the empty cabin. "Along with the body."

"Could be."

"Good Lord."

TWELVE

Thursday Night—
Musket Beach (continued)

AFTER Tony's call, Pat sat on the couch and stared into the barely flickering fire, recalling some of their conversation.

"Along with the body," she'd said.

"Could be."

"Good Lord."

And she felt a chill. Despite her wool black-and-teal plaid slacks and heavy Irish turtleneck, a fine cold shiver of fear moved along the back of her scalp, tingling tiny hairs on the nape of her neck until it finally faded away in quick little ripples down her spine.

"Tony, why aren't you here instead of there," she whispered, "a thousand miles away and more?"

Then Pat stood and out loud she said, "Come on!

You sit here talking on the phone and brooding and let the fire almost burn itself out."

She walked around the coffee table to the wood stove and, kneeling, fed it the last small pieces of alder, shaking her head as she emptied the tall, tan wicker basket. "Damn!" she said, aloud again. "Forgot to bring in more wood!"

Pat picked up the poker and stabbed at the wood in the stove until a few small flames danced and flared, then she took the canvas wood-carrier from the empty basket and started toward the back door. Passing the wall thermostat, which normally operated the cabin's baseboard heater, she gave it a thunk with her middle finger. "Great time for you to screw up, too."

She took her yellow slicker off its peg in the hall and shoved her arms through the sleeves, shifting the wood-carrier from right hand to left to right again on her way to the back door. Peering through the little window, she flipped on the switch to the outside light.

Shocking white light bounced right back, almost blinding her, forcing her to squint for a second at the sudden reflection off the bright white wall of fog drifting across the back deck. The deck itself had a damp sheen, and two steps down, where the fog trailed away, the wet grass sparkled and blinked in the light.

Thirty feet away—dimly, dimly seen along the back fence, black in the fog—a line of wind-warped pines dripped water from long pointed needles onto the four-foot-high stack of firewood they were supposed to be sheltering.

Pat unlocked the door and pulled it open. The metal weatherstripping rasped and screeched in the quiet night and brought a booming answer from the big, deep voice of the black Labrador at the house beyond the fence.

Perhaps it was the door's screech, or the sound of Pat's footsteps across the deck, or her shadow on the fog as she crossed the backyard to the woodpile; perhaps it was her scent; something made the dog bark again. And again. And while Pat filled the carrier with firewood the Lab, sounding much closer on his side of the fence, boomed a quick series of sharp nonstop barks which suddenly became a long, low, rumbling growl.

Pat stopped. Cold chills shivered over her upper arms, across her shoulders, down the middle of her back. She sensed, she *knew*—just as surely as that growling dog knew—that someone else was out there, very near, in the fog. The fingers of her right hand searched along the top of the wet, cold stack of wood until they found a stick of alder that she could use as a club.

Now the dog was just on the other side of the low fence, no more than six feet away, and his growl became the loudest roar Pat had ever heard. She raised her club high, up to her ear, ready to swing, and began backing slowly toward the cabin, trembling, shaking, looking from right to left, eyes wide then squinting, trying to see through the fog.

A man's voice slammed across the woodpile and hit Pat so hard it was like he'd punched her in the belly;

her whole body jerked and her heart almost stopped. "All right, Rowdy, goddammit shut up!" Then the voice became soothing. "C'm'ere, Rowdy, come on. It's all right, boy."

There was sudden quiet. A wind gust shook the pines. Water drops pottled along the wood pile and onto Pat's yellow slicker. The dog began a soft, high, deep-throat whine.

The man spoke, curious this time. "Miz Pratt, is that you over there?"

The soothing voice was somehow familiar, but Pat began backing away again, holding the wood-carrier in her left hand, her club ready in her right. She heard a movement on the other side of the wood pile.

"You okay?" the voice questioned. "Sorry if I and that dog scared you."

Pat continued slowly backward, trying to fit a face to the voice. Dead twigs cracked by the middle pine tree, a branch swished back into place. With the light over the cabin deck behind her, Pat was a silhouette. In front of her, a shadow of movement stirred the bright wall of fog and out of it a dark blob appeared and began to take shape. "It's me, Miz Pratt. Martin Ross."

The shape became a dark, crumpled-crown Stetson, a rain-slick yellow poncho, jeans, boots, and finally the grocer as he stopped ten feet away.

Pat began to breathe again. "Well, Mr. Ross." She sighed. She lowered her club and let her shoulders droop for a second. "For some reason we've been bumping into each other a lot lately, but I never expected anything like this. What are you doing here?"

"Just a little walk." He said it casually, but his hands moved around in the nervous gestures that Pat had noticed before—scrubbing his chin, nudging his glasses back up on his nose, curling along the brim of his hat. "Closed the store a bit ago and wanted some fresh air. Just cuttin' through your side yard when you turned the light on."

Pat had forgotten, with the fright and the adrenalin pumping, why she had come out. His words made her suddenly aware of the weight of the firewood in the carrier hanging from her left hand. She put it down on the glistening wet grass.

"I woulda kept goin' but I thought it might worry you to hear somebody scufflin' along out here in the fog. So I stopped and waited for you to get your wood. Then old Rowdy started barking over there 'n' now we're here 'n' that's that."

"Well," she repeated, with another deep breath. "I certainly wish you had said something right away." She folded her arms across her chest, still holding her club. "And I must say, you seem to have a way with dogs, at least. Or that one must know you pretty well."

"Lived here in Musket Beach a long time, Miz Pratt. Know all the people and most of the dogs in town." He gave a hoarse chuckle. "And I guess you're right that they prob'ly know me, too." He paused, and as he went on his voice became a little less friendly, a little harder. "And one thing everybody *oughta* know: Even if they don't care about me, they know that I care about this town."

Pat nodded. "Yes, that's what I've heard," she said,

frowning a little, as if wondering why she was standing out here in the cold, foggy night talking to, of all people, Martin Ross. "Several people around town have mentioned your devotion to Musket Beach."

"Even if they don't like me, they got to respect the way I work to make this a good place to live. And a nice little place for tourists to come and have a good time and spend a little money."

"Well, it certainly is that, from what I've seen and judging from the crowds in town this weekend."

Ross went on almost as though Pat hadn't said a word. He seemed interested only in his own thoughts, concentrating on making her understand his own point of view. "That's what Musket Beach lives on, mostly, you know, is tourists. There's no logging business around here, to speak of—no mills, no factories, not even a fishing fleet. The business of Musket Beach is *people*— the people who live here, and the people who build or buy vacation homes here, and the tourists, bless 'em— the people that come over here to the coast for a weekend or a holiday or just to visit for a while. That's what we live on. That's the way it's always been, and that's the way I like it." He stopped for a second, then added with a little smile, "I mean to say, that's the way *we* like it. And nothin's gonna change it."

Pat shrugged and, using the hand holding the club, she waved toward Musket Beach. "What about those people marching through town today? Wouldn't there be quite a few changes if they moved in, complete with guru?"

Martin Ross took one small step toward Pat and leaned forward, saying softly, "Miz Pratt, what you see is not *always* what you get." He straightened. "And as far as I'm concerned, the more people, the better for Musket Beach. And now I'll just finish my walk and get on home."

He started to leave but stopped in mid-turn, looking back at Pat.

"Guess you'll be glad when your husband gets back Saturday, hey?"

"You're right about that."

"Thought so." His right hand pushed his glasses up, and continued on to touch the brim of his Stetson. "Well, g'night."

"Good night."

"Hope nobody gets in the way o' that stick you're wavin' around."

He turned and walked away, followed by Rowdy, the now-friendly Lab. And as Martin Ross disappeared into the fog, Pat frowned. There was something he'd said, something that made her shake her head and wonder.

Pat stooped to take up the handles of the wood-carrier and stopped, staring at a bald spot beside it in the damp grass. There, slightly muddy but quite clear, was the imprint of a boot. Its toe was pointing away from the deck, toward the wood pile and the back fence. Someone had been on the deck and then walked away from the cabin.

She quickly lifted the firewood, looked over her

shoulder at the fog which had swallowed Martin Ross, and hurried back to the cabin. Inside, she locked the door and tested it, then reached toward the switch for the outside light. She stopped, nodding her head firmly, and left the light on over the back deck.

She went into the livingroom, put more wood into the stove, and dumped the rest of her load into the tall wicker basket. Still wearing her yellow slicker, she sat on the edge of the coffee table in front of the stove, hunching toward the heat. She stared into the flames for a few moments, eyes narrow, a crease between her brows, worrying her way through that eerie meeting with Martin Ross, trying to understand what he'd said that caused her to worry so.

After a while she gave up, stood and went around the room making sure the windows were locked, closing the blinds, pulling the curtains. She double-checked the lock on the front door and turned on the light over the front deck.

In the kitchen she filled a wine glass with a white Bordeaux, nodded her head again, and poured the wine back into the bottle, dribbling some down the side. She recorked the bottle and put it back in the refrigerator, licking spilled wine off her fingers. "Tasty, but let's have some tea," she muttered, and put the kettle on.

She took off her slicker and hung it on its peg in the hall and went on into the bedroom. She came out carrying a rust colored quilt and a pillow, took them into the livingroom, and arranged them on the couch.

She went back to the bedroom, came out with

Tony's heavy plaid bathrobe and his Navy blue pajamas instead of her own nightgown, and went into the bathroom. A few minutes later she came out of the bathroom wearing pajamas and robe, went into the kitchen, moved the whistling tea kettle to another burner, turned the stove off, and went back to the living-room.

She put another piece of wood in the stove, adjusted the damper, turned off the light, and curled up under the quilt on the couch. After a few minutes she got up, went around the coffee table and picked up the poker, put it on the coffee table by the couch where she could reach it, and crawled under the quilt again.

This time she didn't curl up. She lay stiff and straight, eyes wide open. She stared through the darkness at the flames dancing behind the door of the wood stove, but she saw Martin Ross with the fog drifting around his dark, round shape. She finally remembered what he'd said that made her wonder and worry. "How does Martin Ross know," she said aloud to the empty cabin, "how does he know that Tony won't be back till Saturday?"

THIRTEEN

Friday Morning— Hollywood

AT nine the next morning, waiting for arranger-composer Irwin Jackson, Tony sat with his feet up on the desk in the tiny, cluttered reception room of VoiceBox Recording on Selma Avenue. Small and inexpensive, VoiceBox was built to do just what it said: to record announcers, narrators, and singers who wouldn't be seen on camera.

Jax and a singing group were coming in to overdub the jingle for the radio and TV commercials Tony was producing. Overdubbing—adding singers or an announcer's voice to a prerecorded music track—was strictly against union rules. But the union seemed to overlook overdubbing.

Tony had asked about it in the past, concerned that

it might cause problems for his agency or his clients. "Not to worry," Jax had said. "That's just the way it's done. We know it's against the rules. The unions know we do it. And they know why." He held up a cautionary finger. "Suppose we follow the rules and try to record everybody at the same time—musicians, singers, announcer, actors. And suppose we work till everybody gets it right—not just all those people in the studio but the people in the control booth, too, like the producer *and* the director ..."

"... *and* the writer," Tony had interrupted.

"... *and* the engineer *and* the tape operators—all those people working to get *one take* with no goofs, no mechanical screw-ups, no stutters, no cracked notes, everything in tune and on time—it would take hours and hours and hours. The cost would be *astronomical.* Most clients couldn't afford it. Or wouldn't pay it. Which means that most of these union members would be out of work. Or they'd be working nonunion!" Jax shrugged. "Maybe someday it'll change. But right now, we keep on breakin' the rules, and they keep lookin' the other way. It's crazy."

Now, Tony waited for Jax and the singers to come in and break the rules again. Behind him, the control room door was closed, but the odd squeaks, squawks, yaps, and giggles that leaked through told him that there was an early-morning session in progress.

The phone on the desk rang, one of its three lights blinking rhythmically beside Tony's propped up feet. He started swinging around to answer it but the ringing stopped and the light glowed steadily as someone in the studio picked up the receiver. The sounds from the studio continued a few more seconds, stopped, and suddenly the control room door opened and out came big, round, nearly bald Rolly Nidecker, owner-operator of VoiceBox Recording.

Rolly closed the door, frowning, muttering to himself, "Third g-goddam phone c-call this morning! Even takes calls for his g-girlfriend, for c-chrissakes!" Then he noticed Tony and smiled broadly, holding out a beefy hand. "Hey, T-Tony. You're here!"

Tony swung his feet down, standing to shake Rolly's hand. "I'm here," he said, and at the same moment the street door opened. Tony turned around, squinting at the figure coming through the glaring sunlit rectangle. "And Jax is here, too."

"Hey, Tones. Rolls. What's happening?"

Tony shook hands with Rolly but spoke to Jax. "I don't know. According to the schedule on Rolly's desk, we're the first ones in today. But somebody's already here, and I have the feeling we're about to be put on hold."

Rolly's right hand was warm and sweaty. His left hand nervously unbuttoned another button, the fourth, on his floppy sport shirt. His bloodshot eyes blinked back and forth between Jax and Tony and his big head wagged from side to side. "Listen, c-can I p-put your s-session on hold for a few m-minutes? I've g-g-got . . ."

"Cool it! Cool it!" Jax dropped his briefcase on the desk and grabbed Nidecker's shoulders, looking wor-

111

ried. "Slow down, Rolls, slow down," he said gently, then slowly waved his fingers in front of Nidecker's face. "Take it easy, man. Take a deep breath."

Rolly slumped against the door frame, breathing deeply. Almost visibly, his various body tics eased and he watched with smiling eyes as Jackson began to mimic his gestures and speech. "Y-you're all excited, m-man, and you kn-know what happens when you g-get exc-c-cited."

Jax stopped his imitation and said, "So try some deep breathing."

Rolly Nidecker looked at Tony and dipped his head at Jackson. "Th-think we been workin' t-t-together" he swallowed "too long?"

Jax's gravelly voice cut in quietly, "Less deep thinking and more deep breathing."

After another long inhale Rolly pushed away from the door and went on in his rapid-fire style. "D-dig this, man: we get a crash c-call from N-New York Tuesday m-morning. 'Redo those TV tracks! Right now!' they said. 'And those tapes've g-*got* to be on a plane to New York by Friday night!'"

He paused for more air.

"That's tonight! So I squoze a session in ahead of yours and we're not quite finished. So I need to use a little of your time."

Jackson held up a hand, palm outward. "No problem, man," and he looked at Tony, who nodded. "No problem, just so our job gets done and we're gone by noon."

"No sweat," Rolly smiled. He blew out a breath and took another one in. "Jeez, what a panic! Had to re-book all the talent! Singers! Actors! Jeez! Re-recording all day Wednesday and yesterday and still goin' today! Even had to call Paul on Tuesday night up in Oregon and he had to fly down and . . ."

He stopped, suddenly realizing something. "Hey. It just d-dawned on me." He looked at Tony, then back into the control room, and again at Tony. "I for-g-got. You two g-guys are from the same place!"

"Who're you talking about?" Tony asked.

And another voice said immediately, "Yeah, what two g-guys from what same p-place?"

A short, squat torso appeared from behind Rolly, standing in the glare that burned through the open doorway.

Rolly waved a big hand between Tony and the little man as he said, "Tony P-Pratt, meet P-Paul Taylor."

Tony studied the face squinting into the sunlight; Jax pushed the door and its shadow swung through the room and across Taylor's face, seeming to wipe open the narrowed bright blue eyes. Pink rimmed but not tired, they looked back at Tony from a big head which cocked to the right, like a watching bird. The face, very tan, gave the impression of having been arranged in a frame of tightly permed brick-red curls, graying sideburns, and a full beard, neatly squared and nearly white.

Taylor said it again. "What two guys from what same place?" His voice was not so deep as Jackson's but it was richer, fuller, drawn with an actor's authority out of a thick, broad chest. His torso appeared to rest heavily, precariously, balanced on narrow hips held up by legs as short and thin as baseball bats.

"You two," Rolly Nidecker said. "B-both you g-guys c-came down from Oregon," Rolly said.

The actor's smile beamed big and bright on Tony. "Is that so? From where in Oregon?" He reached out to shake hands.

"Portland."

The red curls nodded.

"And we have a cabin at the coast," Tony added. "At Musket Beach. Know where it is?"

Taylor's lower lids ticked upward once and there was a quick, convulsive squeeze in his handshake, as though some kind of connection had clicked. But the shining white smile didn't falter.

"Know where it *is*? I *live* there! What a coincidence! We'll have to get together after the session."

Taylor dropped Tony's hand, turned, and reached up and grabbed Rolly's shoulders, urging him back toward the control room. At the same time his deep voice became nasal, with a country twang: "Which we gots to finish raht naow 'fore Ah loses me a hu-*mung*-ous account."

Rolly let himself be moved into the control room and then, as Taylor continued past him, he slipped aside and grabbed the door. Before it closed, he shoved his big torso back into the office, popped his eyes wide, and said in a loud stage whisper, "And wait'll you see the talent he b-brought along."

114

"From Oregon?" Jackson sounded as though girls couldn't grow there.

"Yeah. *Some* little town up there." Rolly's face frowned and grinned at the same time in his effort to remember something. "How did Paul say that? Oh, yeah. I'll tell you how 'country' she is: Her hometown's got a three-stool saloon, a two-pump gas station, and a one-hole outhouse."

In the middle of Rolly's cackling laugh, another of Paul Taylor's specialty voices boomed out of the big speakers in the control room—the voice of a happy, high-pressure game show announcer: "No more hemorrhoids! Yes, friends, use Preparation H and kiss your hemorrhoids goodbye!"

Quickly, he changed voices again and a little girl's high, reedy, pleading voice came through. "Come on, Unca Wolly, stop scwewin' awound."

Rolly shook his head, grinning, and started to close the door.

"Hold it!" Jax said. "What about Taylor's chick—the one he brought with him."

"She's gonna p-pick him up in a little b-bit." His lips pursed and he pulled in a long, admiring breath while the fingers of his right hand, spread wide, wagged limply up and down in front of his stomach. "Whoooooey. Name's C-Carole C-Conley."

Rolly closed the door. Tony stood and stared at it, looking stunned. He repeated the name softly to himself, as though it were out of context. "Carole Conley. Could it be? Carole . . . "

"Sounds like a phoney name, Tones."

"Phoney?"

"Like a stage name, right? Right." Jax held his hands up as though framing a picture and boomed out the name like a burlesque announcer. "'Carole Conley!'" He let out a laugh. "Tones, that's a name somebody made up."

Suddenly, Tony was standing on the nighttime beach with Pat. Martin Ross was there, too, and Officer Barrett, and they were all looking down at a body sprawled on the sand. He remembered saying, "Anybody who could make up a name like that can't be all bad." And he remembered the grim response from Ross: "Like a lot of things, the name didn't belong to him, either."

In Hollywood, Tony looked at Jax without seeing him. "So the Musket Beach gossip is true," he said, just barely aloud. "Conley's wife *is* running around with the actor."

"Who're you talking about, Tones?"

"Carl Conley," he said, and shook his head.

"*Carole* Conley," Jackson corrected.

The door to the street flew open and singer Gene Perretti stood in the door frame, backlit by the sunlight and laughing. "How's this for unison effort: All five singers are late, but we all drive into the parking lot at the same time."

As the four other singers came crowding into the little office, Jackson shook his head at Tony and said, "You've lost me on the Conley chick, Tones, so I'm goin' to work."

Jax passed out the vocal parts to the singers, and while they looked them over and hummed and settled themselves, he explained that they'd lost some of their studio time because of Rolly's emergency session. "So let's run through this a few times out here, without the tracks, till we can get in the studio. Right?"

Without looking up from their music, the singers nodded.

"Right," Jax said, spreading his score on the desk with his left hand and raising his right, fingers snapping to set the tempo. "Okay. Spot Number One. Sixty seconds. Everybody got it? Watch out for the pick-up in bar eight. Ready? One—two—one, two, three . . ."

As he had told Pat in the past, what Tony did during music sessions was mostly sit and listen. The major part of his work was already done, long before, in the planning and the writing and in talks with Jax and the other arrangers about timing, styles, instrumentation, tempo, and singers. When it came time to go into the studio, he was there primarily to make cuts or additions in the copy, if that should be necessary, and to work with the announcer on interpretation.

So now he just let Jax and the singers do their work, while his thoughts wandered to Paul Taylor. And Carole Conley. And Carl Conley. On Musket Beach.

Thinking about Taylor, he turned a script over and scrawled notes on the back. Taylor had been faking about something during their introduction—Tony knew it. Taylor had reacted to Tony's name the moment Musket Beach was mentioned; that's what caused the sharp little flick around Taylor's eyes and the quick pressure in his handshake. This wild coincidence of meeting in Los Angeles, even booking the same studio on the same day, had probably blocked the connection from Taylor's mind, momentarily. But then, if Taylor *did* link Tony with Musket Beach, why would he keep acting otherwise, especially after they had established mutual residence? Why not make the usual kind of response, something like, "So that's where I've heard your name!"

That was another side of the puzzle. Where had Taylor heard Tony's name? From whom? There was very little chance that Taylor had heard about Tony through the advertising business; it usually worked the other way: there were always a lot of anonymous writers and producers wandering around, but there were very few people with Paul Taylor's talent.

Besides, the connection clicked in Taylor's mind— and he reacted—when Tony mentioned Musket Beach. And there was only one link between Tony, Paul Taylor, and Musket Beach. That link was Carl Conley. Or, rather, Carl Conley's body. Which implied that Taylor was involved somehow with Conley's death.

Now. Assuming *that,* how did Taylor know that Tony knew anything about it?

He and Pat had found—discovered—the body on Tuesday night; Wednesday, they had been at the cabin, except for his half-an-hour or so at the police station; Thursday, he had driven home to Portland, then to the airport to catch the flight to Burbank; and Pat, he was sure, hadn't talked to anyone else about finding the body until her conversation in the bookstore, by which time Taylor was already here in Hollywood.

So. Had someone in Musket Beach telephoned Taylor?—possibly one of those calls Rolly was grumbling about—and told Taylor about Tony? Who could it have been? Who else had seen Tony standing over Carl Conley's body, and might have told Paul Taylor about it?

There was the ambulance crew, who lived fifteen miles away and wouldn't know Taylor from a stack of clam shells.

There was the jogger, with her dog, whose family had come from Idaho for the Sand Castle contest.

There was Officer Barry Barrett, the close-mouthed cop who played things very close to his vest. Barrett was the only person in Musket Beach, besides Pat, who knew Tony's schedule.

And Martin Ross, the grocer. What was behind that "leading man" remark he'd made, standing over Carl Conley's body? Was there more to it than Barrett had let on? And was there more than one person from Musket Beach doing some acting?

Tony paused. Then, remembering, he muttered "Ah" to himself and went on making notes.

The driver of the car that raced away: What about him? Or, possibly, her?

And just as important: What about the "why?" Why would a small-town real estate dealer wind up dead on the beach? Was something going on behind the scenes in that small town?—something so bad that it could lead to murder?

At that moment, the studio door and the street door burst open simultaneously but everybody in the little office stared at the street door.

All five singers stopped rehearsing—stopped cold, with their mouths open.

Jax s head snapped around and his glasses skidded down his nose.

Rolly Nidecker and Paul Taylor came out of the studio, and Rolly let go with a hog-caller's "whoooo-EEE!"

Tony knocked the scripts off his lap.

Taylor smacked his hands together and laughed a deep, rolling laugh.

Silhouetted in the doorway stood the most perfectly proportioned woman Tony had ever seen, standing slender and straight, her long legs spread, hands on hips. The bright sun behind her lit an auburn halo in her hair and lent a golden California glaze to her bare shoulders and arms. The sunlight seemed to blaze around her body and through her filmy, gauzy, knee-length dress as though she wore nothing at all.

She glanced around the room at everyone looking back and, with a sudden husky laugh, she bent forward and down, her long hair tossing in the light, and looked back through her legs. Still bent forward, she raised her head and grinned through her tumbled hair at Taylor. "I *knew* it! Pauly, you can see right *through. That*'s why you bought me this dress!"

Then she straightened and her left hand swept her glistening hair over her head again.

"Okay, how 'bout this?" She spun quickly, profile, pressing her straight back against the door frame, seeming to lay against the frame, leaning, lifting her left leg to let the spike-heeled sling pump rest on her right knee; she held a deep, deep breath to swell her belling breasts. The sunlight behind her burned a kind of aura along every long, tapering line, every angle, every curve.

Awed silence filled the little room for about five seconds, then cracked in several pieces.

Jackson called to the singers, "Okay, folks, let's go do some work," and they scooped up their music and headed for the studio door, crowding through past Rolly.

Rolly, eyes popped out, whumped his big hands together applauding and cheering the girl's silhouette.

Taylor spread his arms wide, swept across the room, and wrapped them around her waist, pulling her upright and pushing himself against her. His permed curls just barely topped her cleavage as he grazed across its crest.

Laughing, wriggling, she pulled him tighter. "There's my little big man!"

Tony sat and watched them as if his pants were glued to his chair, leaning across his open briefcase to pick up the script pages sprayed around his feet. The briefcase tumbled from his lap, clattering on the floor as more sheets of paper fluttered down around it.

Reaching for it, he still had his head turned toward the girl and Taylor, whose nose and mouth gently wandered through her cleavage with little sniffs and moans. The actor, scarcely interrupting his snuffling, cocked one eyelid and looked up at her as he said, "By the way—and why I think of it now, I don't know—but your friendly neighborhood grocer called again and . . ."

He stopped and stood absolutely still, leaning into the girl, before turning his head slowly toward Tony. Through one slitted eye, he looked across her left breast.

"Oh," he said quietly, "yes," and resettled his nose in its nest. He wagged his curls once toward Tony. "Mr. Graceful, here," he went on, in a slightly muffled voice, "is also from Oregon."

Her eyes, still laughing, followed Taylor's gesture and looked at Tony, reading him up and down as he introduced himself. "Tony. Tony Pratt."

"Carole," she said, mocking his phrasing and intonation. "Carole Conley." She looked away, then back again. "That's Carole with an 'e'."

"Which you'll have to admit," said Taylor, without looking up, "is a considerable improvement over CarolMae, which is what it used to be. CarolMae Arp."

She tapped him once on the top of his head and put on a playful pout. "Pauly. You said you wouldn't tell."

Taylor suddenly raised his head. Cupping his right hand behind his right ear, in burlesque imitation of announcers on old-time radio soap operas, he spoke in a deep, intimate voice using her left breast as a microphone. "Welcome once again to the story of

CarolMae Arp, the story that asks the question: Can this little girl from a small logging town in Ory-gawn find happiness as a budding real estate tycoon. And speaking of buds . . ." and he dipped his nose back toward her cleavage.

"Pauly, Pauly you nut." Giggling gently, Carole draped her left hand over Taylor's shoulder and held her right hand on the back of his head, moving it gently from side to side between her breasts as she gazed straight ahead. Her chin lifted, resting on top of Taylor's curls, and she closed her eyes.

"Tony Pratt," she continued, in nursery rhyme rhythm, "Tony Pratt would eat no fat."

"No, no," Taylor said, his voice muffled, "Tony Pratt, with a wife named Pat."

Tony looked at him sharply, then asked the girl, "Do you live in Musket Beach, too?"

"At the moment."

Slowly, Tony said, "Conley. Conley. By any chance related to *Carl* Conley?"

"Well! What a surprise," she smiled, eyebrows raised. "So you know old Numb Nuts!"

Taylor, his nose buried between her breasts, blew a smothered snort.

Tony's eyebrows shot up and he blurted out, "Who?"

"Carl Conley. My husband."

CHAPTER

FOURTEEN

Friday Morning—
Hollywood (continued)

Tony looked punchy, out of it. He slumped in a chair beside Rolly Nidecker at the console in VoiceBox Recording's control room. Watching but not really seeing, he stared across the narrow room and through the glass wall of a tiny ten-foot-square studio. On the other side of the soundproof glass, Irwin Jackson and the five singers crowded together around a boom mike in a tight circle of music stands. Wearing headsets, through which Rolly played back the music track, they sang the jingle with the music for the first time.

During these rehearsals, the loudspeakers in the control room were turned off. So, the singers were singing but no sound came out of the studio. The glass wall gave it the appearance of a square goldfish bowl, and inside the bowl Jax frantically waved his arms in

125

the air, keeping time, throwing cues, conducting an eager, enthusiastic, apparently voiceless choir. With their headphones clamped on and their eyes bugged out as they concentrated on sight-reading, with their mouths opening and closing in silent unison, the singers looked like a rare and exotic species of fish. "Very tall, very hairy tuna," Tony muttered.

Rolly looked at him, sideways. "Huh?"

"I said, 'This can be a silly business.'"

Rolly nodded. "I'm hip."

Tony tried to bring his mind to the recording session but he kept hearing Carole Conley's answer, seeing Taylor immediately sweep up her twenty-five-year-old beautiful body and carry her out the door and across the sidewalk and plop her onto the passenger seat of his top-down Rolls Corniche.

"Carole with an 'e'," she'd said. Half Carl Conley's age and at least four times as much as he could handle.

Carl Conley's wife. Widow, really. But apparently she didn't know it, judging from her answer. Present tense, not past. "So you know old Numb Nuts."

Maybe she didn't know that her husband was dead. Or maybe she didn't care. She was obviously having a great time playing around Hollywood with Taylor. The little man had a big reputation. He made bags of money and he spent it with a flair: Exclusive restaurants, expensive wines, exotic cars. Like the Rolls Corniche.

Which made Tony wonder. If Taylor's Hollywood car was so distinctive, what kind of car did he have in Musket Beach? Was it as recognizable as the Rolls?

Which brought back Pat's idea: The night they found the body, did Officer Barrett recognize the car that raced away?

Pat.

How had Taylor known her name? "No, no," he'd muttered across the top of Carole Conley's cleavage, "Tony Pratt, with a wife named Pat."

Either Taylor had made a lucky, flukey guess trying to find a fast rhyme, or he knew Pat's name from one of the two people who knew she'd been there on the beach with Tony. One was a grocer. The other was a cop. And one of those two must be playing games, either with Carole Conley or with Paul Taylor. Or both.

And what was that remark of Taylor's?—something he'd started to say to Carole Conley. "Your friendly neighborhood grocer called again . . ." And suddenly he'd stopped, glancing at Tony, without saying anything more. What did that mean? Was Ross the "friendly, neighborhood grocer" who was on such good terms with Carole Conley that he knew where to call her in Hollywood?

Or was it *Taylor* that Ross had called? Was Ross involved with the little actor in Carl Conley's death? If so, did it mean that Pat—alone in Musket Beach—was in some kind of danger from Ross?

And if there *was* any danger for Pat, what about Officer Barrett?—could he be relied on for help? Or, since he didn't follow the car that left the scene, could Barrett be mixed up in this and, in that case, no help for Pat?

127

Abruptly, Tony got up and bumped around Rolly's chair, reaching for the telephone at the other side of the console.

He dialed a number and waited, listening to the dull burr of the phone ringing at least twenty times in the cabin at Musket Beach. Where was Pat? On the beach? Shopping? Gallery-hopping?

He rattled the phone back into its cradle and looked at his watch, thinking of Pat and her morning routine at the beach. Whenever possible, she liked to linger over a late breakfast, her morning coffee, her newspaper, her crossword puzzle. "And maybe one more half-piece of toast," she'd say.

Tony began talking to himself. "Ordinarily, she wouldn't leave the cabin at this time of day—not at ten or ten-thirty in the morning." He reached for the telephone again and dialed. "Maybe I had the wrong number."

Rolly, rolling a new reel of blank tape onto an eight-track recording machine alongside the console, looked over at Tony. "Are you talkin' to m-me?"

"Me?" Tony listened to the maddening burr-burr-burr coming back from Musket Beach. "No. Didn't even know I was talking."

He held the phone another twenty rings before he slammed it down and went back and fell into his chair. Where was Pat? What the hell was going on! How did Taylor know Pat's name? How did Carole Conley *not* know her husband was dead? Why didn't Barrett, the slick cop, tell Tony that he *knew* Taylor was playing around with Conley's wife?

Grabbing his notebook he headed for the phone once more and picked it up, thumbing through his book. He found the number and dialed.

Two rings. Then, "Musket Beach Police."

The words rushed out of Tony's mouth, "This is Tony Pratt calling Officer Barrett, is he in?"

"Hi, Mr. Pratt. You back? This is only Friday morning. I thought you'd still be in L.A."

"I'm still down here," Tony hurried on, "and I need a favor."

"You sound pretty stirred up."

"I just tried to call my wife and there's no answer at the cabin and I wonder if you'd stop by and see if everything's all right."

"Well, I don't think you have anything to worry about. She looked all right when I saw her earlier this morning."

"You saw her? This morning?"

"On her way up to Paul Taylor's place. You know, the actor I was tellin' you about? The one that—"

"Yes, yes, I know," Tony cut in. "What was she doing there?"

"I don't know, I didn't stop. But I knew she wouldn't see Taylor."

"Why is that?"

"He left Tuesday night. Early Wednesday morning, really. One of the Seashore officers was making his nightly check on that little airstrip up there when Taylor took off."

"Took off?"

"Yeah. Took off. In his airplane."

"He has his own plane?"

"Sure. He's in and out o' that little airport all the time."

Rewinding the music tracks, Rolly Nidecker switched on the loudspeakers. At that instant, a thousand-cycle tone rolled past the playback heads and the high, piercing tone screamed off the tape, through the speakers, through the telephone into Officer Barrett's ear. It hit Barrett so hard he almost jumped through the phone. "What's that? Mr. Pratt! You okay?"

Rolly punched a button to stop the tape just as Jax pushed open the studio door and walked across the control room, frowning at Tony. "Hey, Tones, you look bad, man. What's happenin'?"

FIFTEEN

Friday Morning—
The Cabin, Musket Beach

ON Friday morning, out of a deep sleep, Pat's eyes popped wide open when she felt cold, cold metal against her right hand. She blinked, looking around to make sure of her surroundings.

She was at the beach cabin. On the couch. Under the quilt. She was snarled up in Tony's big plaid bathrobe, and her right hand had flopped over the side of the couch and hit the cold handle of the poker on the coffee table beside her.

She brought both hands under the quilt and rubbed them together for warmth, shivering as she remembered last night and the woodpile and the barking dog and Martin Ross. She looked around at the buff-colored curtains drawn across the windows; it was still dark on the ocean side of the cabin but looking bright and promising on the east side where the sun was just clearing the hilltops.

Pat untangled herself from the bedding. She sat up, yawning and scratching her rump, glancing at the Dax clock on the wall. "Ten after seven," she said aloud. "Guess I wasn't too nervous to sleep, once I got there."

She built up the fire in the wood stove and went about her morning routine, which today included one egg over easy, rye toast with Grand Maman Greengage Preserves, and decaffeinated mocha java.

Added to her rounds this morning were three extra trips to the woodpile; she crammed wood into the tall wicker basket by the stove and when it was full she stacked more wood behind it.

Finally she carried a director's chair out to the front deck and sat down, face to the sun, sneakers up on the railing, and finished her crossword puzzle. That done, she got a pad of paper, another cup of coffee, and one more half-piece of toast and started a "Things To Do Today" list.

Her first note on the lined yellow pad was:

Fourth of July. Salute!

This was followed by:

Weekend meals
Saturday Dinner: Out!
(But just in case—Martha's Company Casserole)

132

Friday Morning

Shopping: Noodles
          Hamburger
          Cottage Cheese
          Stewed Tomatoes

Sunday Lunch: Here—Soup & Fruit
          Dinner: Home (stop @ store on way)

A series of doodling O's, loops, and arrows filled the next couple of lines. Then:

Why M. Ross in backyard last night?
Why "   " driving car past cabin Thurs. P.M.?
Why "   " behind me at bank Thurs. A.M.?

WHY M. ROSS?!!!
What about note seen on Ross' desk, night of
   body:

Martin—
                Guru says OK!
                CC

To Police Station—tell Officer Barrett about note.

See Paul Taylor?

Pat paused and looked up from her writing and out toward the ocean, white-rimmed at the shoreline, broad and blue beyond. A frown worried across her forehead and she rubbed both palms on the arms of her chair before she looked down and wrote after her last note·

133

Why? To see studio? To see if editing block is
   missing?

Why are we getting involved in this?
Because we found body?
To show we didn't have anything to do with
   murder?
To use as background for another story?
Because it's the Fourth of July and
THIS IS THE AMERICAN WAY?

B.S.

   She stood up and stretched, looking at her watch.
"Ten-of-the-clock," she said aloud. "Let's move it."
   And she ripped the note off the pad, stuffed it in
her pocket, and went inside to dress for a trip to town.

CHAPTER

SIXTEEN

Friday Morning— Hollywood (continued)

TONY banged the phone down and cut off Barrett's questions, then dropped into his chair again, not noticing that Irwin Jackson and the singers had come out of the small studio. For several seconds his dull eyes roamed around Rolly Nidecker's control room, not seeing how worried Rolly, Jax, and the singers were. And it was a long time before he responded to Jax's nervous questions. "Hey, Tones, you okay? What's happening?"

Finally, with a little groan, Tony said softly, "I wish I knew, Jax. I wish I knew what's going on."

Then he sat up and turned to Rolly at the mixing console. "Paul Taylor flies his own plane down here? From Musket Beach?"

Smiling, the big engineer nodded. "L-lots of t-times."

"This time?"

"Yeah. Came in Wednesday m-morning."

"Where does he come in? Burbank? L.A. International?"

Rolly nodded again. "L.A.X."

"Do you know what kind of plane it is? How fast?"

Rolly spread his arms and grinned. "All I know is, it s cool, m-man. V-very cool."

Tony smashed his hand down on the console and everybody jumped. "Come on, Rolly!" he shouted, "I need information, not bullshit!" Then he looked up at the others staring at him.

He held his right hand out in a peaceful gesture toward Rolly and bowed his head for a second. "Sorry. But something's going on. I don't know what. But Paul Taylor's involved, and it may involve my wife."

"Your wife? And Taylor?" Jax laughed. "Listen, man, any woman named Pat who would marry a man named Pratt has *got* to be straight." The two blonde singers nodded and laughed, too.

"Believe me," Jax went on, "she's not foolin' around with Taylor. *You* know that."

"I know! I know!" Tony suddenly dropped his head to his chest and squeezed his eyes shut. "Jesus, what do I have to do to get a straight answer around here?" He looked up again. "That's not what I meant. But I *need* information."

Turning to Rolly, he asked, "Do you know how long it takes for Taylor to fly down from Musket Beach?"

"Ab-b-bout six." Responding to a gesture from Jax, Rolly took a couple of deep breaths and sat back, relaxed, letting his shoulders and arms droop.

"Six hours?"

Rolly nodded. "P-paul says there's usually a tail-wind. B-but it changes this time of year, he says. Goin' the other way he'll hit a headwind, so he figures it'll take about seven hours to get b-back today."

"Back! Today?" Tony almost jumped out of his chair. "Taylor's flying back to Musket Beach *today?*"

"I'm hip, man. I couldn't b-believe it m-myself!" Rolly was getting agitated again. "It's w-wild! D-dig this: I had him b-booked to cut the sound track for a TV p-pilot! A new animated show!"

He looked from Jax to Tony, shaking his head and drawing a circle around the studio with his right index finger. "This afternoon. Right here!" Rolly shook his head sadly. "B-big bread, man, b-but he takes off!"

Tony wagged his head, only partly in sympathy for Rolly and his lost recording fees. "Why would he cancel a date like that? Must be something very important."

"Tell me!" Rolly said, disgusted. He swiveled his chair around to face the mixing console and smacked a button. The two big reels on the machine behind him began to revolve and the silent tape leader started moving across the playback heads, several inches ahead of the first notes of the music track.

"Speaking of dates, Tones," Jax said, herding the singers toward the studio door, "we've got work to do if you want out of here by noon."

Tony nodded, just as the music track powered out

of the big speakers at full, ear-splitting volume. He slapped his hands over his ears and, without looking around, Rolly immediately lowered the gain on the monitors.

"More!" Tony shouted. "More!" And he kept saying it until the sound level was low enough for nearly normal conversation over the music. Only then did he take his hands away from his ears.

"You always want it so *low!*" Rolly complained, hovering over the dials, an exasperated expression on his big, sad face. "How can you mix it if you can't hear it!"

Tony answered with a grin, "I hear it. Believe me." He paused a moment.

"Now, about Taylor. He didn't tell you why he cancelled his session? Or why he wanted to get back to Oregon so fast?"

"Not a word!" Rolly's head bobbed with the beat of the music track and his eyes danced back and forth from the dials and needles on his mixing console to Jax and the singers in the studio.

"Well," he added, as if starting to correct himself. Then he stopped, listening to the singers. He cocked his head, motioned to Jax to move the tenor closer to the mike, listened again, and nodded to Jax. "Well," he continued to Tony, "he *did* say he was sorry if it cost me some bread, but he'd try to make it up to me." He shrugged. "That's all. Mostly we just worked. Or he talked on the phone." Then he chuckled. "Or he talked about the little lady he brought with him."

"You knew that the little lady was married, didn't you?" Tony asked.

Rolly rocked back in his chair and laughed out loud. "No! So *that's* what he meant!"

"About what?"

Still smiling, Rolly went on. "One thing he said was, 'A wife can cause a lot of trouble. Especially if she's not yours.'" He laughed again. "So the Conley chick is married, hey?"

Tony didn't laugh or smile. What if one of Taylor's phone calls was from Martin Ross in Musket Beach? What if the wife Taylor referred to was Pat?

He stood and ducked his head sideways toward the studio and then nodded to Rolly. The engineer smiled and turned the speakers up full blast, till the room rang with music.

Tony grabbed his notebook, held his closed left hand to his ear in a telephoning gesture to Rolly, and went out into the little office, closing the door behind him for comparative quiet.

The third airline he called had a flight to Portland from Burbank in two hours. He took it. He dialed the hotel and asked the cashier to get his bill ready right away. Then he had the call transferred and asked Abe Arthur to come down to Rolly's for this session and to cover the dubbing session for him tomorrow. Then he transferred to Gary Bonham's room to tell the agency manager what he was doing. There was no answer.

And there was no answer when he tried to call Pat. Again.

139

SEVENTEEN

Friday Morning—
Taylor's Place, Musket Beach

PAT found Paul Taylor's house with no help from Tony. "Big place north of town," he'd said, quoting Barrett. "The one with all the land behind it. On the south side of Mount Kenai."

The listing in the telephone book was equally bare: "Taylor, P." and the number. No address.

So Pat went to the one place in town where everyone goes, sooner or later.

The Musket Beach drugstore—*the* Musket Beach drugstore—sat back from the sidewalk on Main Street in a small frame building painted pale green. It had its own step-up wooden sidewalk and its own slanted wooden roof. It even had its own logo etched into the frosted glass front door: a vial of generic valium set in the center of a circle shaped by the words The Musket

Beach Pharmaceutical Company. Straightened out, the name would have been about as long as Main Street.

Pat pushed the door open and smiled up at the old-fashioned bell tinkling above it. She stepped into a square buff-colored room. Drifting across it, near the low ceiling, a thin haze of smoke carried intertwined scents of rose hip tea and cinnamon incense. The tight pinching sound of a sitar drifted through with the smoke and clashed with the jingling ring when Pat closed the door. Behind the counter, a paisley drape parted and a thin, broad-faced young woman stepped through. Her short black hair shone prettily under the track lighting. She and Pat nodded, trading half-smile greetings.

Among the bright yellow Dr. Scholl's packets and the multicolored deodorant cartons, Pat found a box of Q-Tips and a bottle of aspirin and carried them to the counter. She held out a bill with one hand and looked down to drop her wallet into her purse. The clerk's hand cupped hers gently, taking the money. The clerk quickly made change and, her eyes dancing over Pat's face and figure, began counting it, in a whisper, and dropping it slowly into her palm.

Pat smiled and said, "My husband asked me to take some scripts to Paul Taylor's house but I've forgotten the address. Do you know it?"

The rest of her change suddenly plopped into Pat's hand and the young woman's eyes became as hard and flat as her voice. "His address is two-five-two Cedar. And ain't it amazin' how the broads chase that rich little fart?"

Pat's eyes turned cold, too, but her smile stayed sunny and bright. "Thank you. And remember to write to your mother—she must be very proud of you."

Cedar Street turned out to be a winding graveled road traversing Mount Kenai's southern flank at the north end of Musket Beach, on the ocean side of Main Street.

Streets cross Main, generally, east to west; Main runs, generally, north to south. But local topography can cause a street's direction to vary considerably. For example, Main Street points south as straight as a pool cue through the four blocks of the business district, but then it suddenly curls in wide-swinging esses around hills and through ravines on its way through the rest of the town. And there's no grid system. In fact, there's no system at all. As the mailman had said to Pat one day in the post office, "This town didn't grow, it just accumulated."

Pat drove the Volvo wagon up Cedar Street, passing two houses. Side by side, in front of each house, stood two posts. Nailed to one side of each post was a yellow plastic box provided by *The Portland Oregonian* to keep the newspaper dry. On the other side of the post hung a big gray metal mailbox with the street address painted on in black numbers. The first box was numbered 42. The next was 158.

Driving past a patch of wild blackberry vines and escallonia bushes, Pat came to 159.

Then, curving up and around a stand of old-growth cedar and fir, she found herself at the foot of a blacktop driveway leading to the right, away from the road and up a gentle grade to a bench on the side of Mount Kenai. Cedar Street went on straight ahead toward the Pacific and then, according to a county sign on the shoulder in front of her, ended in a turnaround and viewpoint ("No Camping") at the edge of a bluff about fifty yards farther on.

There were no other houses ahead of her, on either side of the road. And here, at the foot of the driveway, there was no post, no newspaper box, and no mailbox with a house number painted on it. But stenciled across the foot of the black driveway, making it look like the end of an airport runway, were the huge, white block numerals 2 5 2.

Pat let the car roll back down the hill a few feet past the blacktop before she accelerated into a hard right turn onto the driveway. At the same moment, the Musket Beach police car came over the rise from the turnaround. Officer Barrett skidded to a stop on the gravel, watching Pat drive up the steep drive and waving as she stuck an arm out her window to wave back at him. Then he drove on.

The driveway flattened out at the house and continued in a loop around it, coming back to join itself in a wide parking area by the front steps. After she started to follow the loop around the house, Pat shook her head, backed up, and parked by the front steps.

She dug in her purse, feeling for comb and lipstick, then reached up and twisted the rear-view mirror so that she could see herself. Combing and touching up, she muttered, "Now what? What do I say if he's in there? 'Hi, I'm here to ask if you killed that man with your editing doohicky.'

"Perfect.

"Or:

"'Hi, my husband told me all about your TV work and I just wanted to tell you how much I enjoy you as the voice of the Jolly Green Doughboy. Or the Pillsbury Giant. Morris the Rat?'"

Her voice turned flat and dry. "Wonderful."

When Pat finished with her lipstick, she squinched her lips together and then checked her teeth for lipstick smears. Then she looked herself in the eye, fluttered her eyelids and said, "Mr. Taylor, so *many* people have told me *so much* about your *charming* home that I just *had* to come and *see* it for *myself!*"

She flipped the lipstick a few inches into the air, snatched it back and dropped it into her bag.

"Ha!" she said with a grinning, satisfied waggle of her head. "That's it!"

Pat got out of the car and looked up at the large, gray-shingled house. She moved along to the corner for another perspective. From this angle there were no other houses in sight. She crossed to the opposite corner. Acre after acre of forest, meadow, and mountainside rolled away from the sides and back of the house. And in front lay a breath-catching view of the beach, the foaming breakers, and the Pacific Ocean's long, slow-motion swell spreading blue forever under the cloudless sky.

145

The house itself had a very contemporary look and feel, but at the same time its weathered exterior seemed to fit naturally in its setting among the rough gray alders and the wrinkled brown Douglas Firs on the sea cliff. Except for the intrusive blacktop drive, the house was perfectly in place, right down to the railroad-tie steps and the wide veranda.

Taking a deep breath, Pat climbed the front steps, walked across, and pushed the bell buzzer. And again. And a third long time. There was no response, no answering step on the other side of the door, no voice.

She walked along the veranda. Through big many-paned windows she looked into a very neat, very masculine livingroom with heavy leather furniture and a deep gray carpet, then into the dining room, where ladderback chairs sat in line around a thick refectory table, polished and gleaming in the sunlight.

Turning away from the dining room window Pat stopped, quickly, as though sensing some faint flicker of movement inside the house, or perhaps a shadow outside from a passing cloud or a gull. She took a step, paused again looking right and left, decided no, and walked on.

Around the corner of the house, the next room was Taylor's little recording studio. Against the far wall stood a pair of tall upright tape recording machines, each with two large silver-colored metal spools on its front. On a long narrow table to the right sat a control board. There was a chair behind the control board, and hanging over the chair was a microphone, suspended

146

from a small boom. A squat, square metal cabinet with a turntable on top stood at the left of the chair, a cassette deck to the right.

Sitting directly under the window was a smaller tape machine, this one with the reels on top. As Pat looked through the window, sunlight poured over her shoulder and across the machine. The light, playing across the smooth metal surface, picked out and highlighted a rough, scuffed patch between the two reels.

Pat bent down for a closer look through the window and as she made the movement she gasped and almost screamed at the reflection of the man standing right behind her.

She spun around, standing straight, blazing. "Goddam you, Martin Ross, you sonofabitch!" She charged after him, swinging her bag like a mace, shouting, "What the hell are you following me around for, scaring the hell out of me!"

Ross' voice was a nervous squeak. "Easy, Miz Pratt, easy." As he backed along the veranda in short, bouncing steps, his fat arms made little pushing motions toward Pat. "Go easy, now. Go easy."

"Don't 'easy' *me*, you sneaky little bastard!" Pat was a storm, furious, forcing Ross back across the porch. Fierce, angry tears flooded her eyes, her face was tight with rage. "What're you *doing!*"

Backing away, Ross reached the steps and stumbled backwards, hooking an arm around the porch pillar as he fell to his knees on the second step.

Pat bent over him panting hard, short breaths.

"You're lucky I don't have a club *now*. Now answer me! What the hell are you *doing* here?!"

He looked up at Pat, his glasses dangling from one ear. "Mr. Taylor. He—uh—he asked me to keep an eye on the place."

Ross slid down another step and got to his feet, fumbling with his glasses, brushing the knees of his plaid slacks, trying to pull himself together. "You know, I could ask *you* the same thing, Miz Pratt." He straightened and looked up at Pat, two steps above him. "What're *you* doin' here?"

"I came to see this house and don't change the subject." Her anger began to ebb a little, but she still swung out emphatically and nearly bashed Ross with her purse as he slid away sideways along the step. "You drive up and down the road in front of our place; you follow me into the bookstore; you follow me into the bank; you're in my back yard at night and . . ." Her rage revived. "You're on my back porch! *At night!* Probably peeking through the window! Just what the hell's the *matter* with you!"

Pat tore at him again, standing over him on the porch, driving Ross across the wide stairway till he leaned backwards over the banister to duck the swinging purse.

"Miz Pratt. Please. Will you please put that thing away and slow down?"

"*Answer me!*"

"I'm just tryin' to keep an eye on you, that's all."

"You're sure as hell doing *that*. Now *Why?*"

148

"'Cause I was worried."

"Worried? *You re* worried! About what?"

"Well, you and Mr. Pratt bein' the ones that found Carl Conley's body—well, it could be that whoever did that to him might do that to you."

EIGHTEEN

Friday Noon— Musket Beach Police Station

OFFICER Barrett leaned forward, elbows on his desk. Hands together, with fingers interlaced and thumbs circling around each other he said, "That doesn't sound like much of a threat to me, Mrs. Pratt."

"Martin Ross didn't *say* it to you. He said it to *me*, dammit! Excuse me, but that man has made me *very* angry. *And* nervous. It sounded like a threat to me. That's why I got away from there as quickly as I could. And that's why I came *here.*"

Sitting in the folding chair alongside Barrett's little gray desk Pat leaned forward, too, back straight, hands on knees, sneakers flat on the floor. "That's *one* of the reasons I came here."

Barrett sat back again and his chair, his belt, and

his holster squeaked as he swiveled around to face Pat. "I've known Martin Ross quite a while and I've never known him to hurt anyone."

"He's a pain to me!"

"Now, now." Barrett stroked the air in a calm-down gesture. "I know you're upset, but try to hear what I'm saying." He folded his hands together on his belt buckle. His voice, quiet and calm, carried over the occasional raspy call on the police radio and the office clatter that came through the door opening into the City Hall. "Ever since his wife died—five, maybe six years ago—Musket Beach has been the main thing in Martin Ross' life. Oh, he's got his store, of course, but his son and daughter-in-law pretty much take care of that, now. So mostly," Barrett shrugged, "this little town is the biggest thing in the world to him. So he wouldn't hurt anybody in it. All he wants is to see it grow!"

"Wouldn't you say that it's a little strange for a city father to be sneaking around and scaring people?"

"What I would say is that I think he really *was* trying to protect you, to be close by in case anything happened, to be ready to help in the event of further activity by person or persons unknown. Because nobody around here knows who or what killed Conley."

"You don't know?"

"We know he was killed by a thump on the head, but we don't what thumped it. In fact, the medical examiner says Conley could've fell and hit his head and killed himself."

Pat's back twitched a little. She crossed her legs.

She rested her left elbow on the desk. "Is that all? Are you getting any help with this?"

"The state police are sending somebody over from Salem, and the county coroner's with the medical examiner right now. They're working on that little piece of metal your husband turned in."

"Oh!" Pat tapped her hand on the desk, suddenly reminded. "The little metal block. Know what it is?"

Surprised at her animated interruption, Barrett shook his head. "No idea."

"It's an editing block."

"It's a what?"

She smiled. "That's what *I* said. It's an editing block. People use it when they cut and splice recording tape. Tony told me about it when he called last night."

Barrett raised his eyebrows for a second. "I wonder why he didn't mention it when I talked to him this morn ... Oh, yes. Your husband called earlier, looking for you."

Pat sat back. "Tony? Called here? For me? Why would he call a police station looking for me?"

Barrett's mustache twitched around a small grin. "Beats me."

Remembering where she was, Pat smiled in return. "This is a rare occasion, believe me." Then she went on, serious, wondering. "And it's funny for him to call in the morning, too. He usually calls in the afternoon or evening. What did he say?"

"Seemed to be worried 'cause you weren't home."

She glanced at her watch. "Almost eleven o'clock," she said, nodding her head. "True. When we're at the beach I'm ordinarily a slow starter, not out and about much in the morning."

"I told him that I'd seen you and you were okay. Told him you were at Taylor's place. He got a little testy about that. Then, when I told him Taylor has an airplane, he really got shook up for some reason." Barrett shrugged. "Anyway, he didn't leave a message. Now. You were sayin' about that metal piece . . . ."

"About the metal block. I think I know where it came from." Pat told him about seeing the tape machine in Taylor's recording studio and about the rough spots on the top of the machine, where something had been glued to the surface and then removed. "And Tony told me last night that you almost need a hammer to knock one of those things loose."

Policeman Barrett shifted in his chair, belt and holster squeaking again. "So what are you suggesting?"

It was Pat's turn to shrug. "I don't know. Maybe someone fell and hit his head against it. Maybe there was a fight and he was *thrown* against it. Maybe he cracked his head so hard it killed him." She paused, then echoed Barrett's earlier comment. "Maybe that's what thumped it." She shuddered. "And, maybe that knocked the metal piece loose. Then maybe the killer picked it up when he took the body out of the studio. And then, maybe, he dropped it accidentally when he dropped the body on the beach." A silence. "I don't know. Could that happen?"

Barrett had watched her carefully all through her theory. Now he looked away for a few moments, thinking, before he looked back and said, "Maybe." He reached for his phone as he added, "And maybe I'll give the state and county people a couple of your ideas."

Pat ducked her head and dug in her pocket as he began to dial. "One more thing," she said. Her voice was unexpectedly hoarse, and louder than usual. Barrett put the phone down as she cleared her throat and handed him a slip of paper.

"What's this?" he asked, unfolding the note.

"I don't know."

He stopped and looked at her. "You got more 'I don't knows' and 'maybes' than one of my kids," he muttered harshly, before reading the note aloud. 'Martin, Guru says OK!' Signed, 'CC'." He kept his head down, looking at the note as he muttered, "S'pose that's the guru that put on the little show for us?" Then his eyes looked up at Pat and he said, louder, "Yeah, your husband showed this to me. Tell me again where you got it? And when?"

"The night we found the body. It was on Martin Ross' desk when I went to his house."

"Mrs. Pratt!" he said, sarcastically, "Don't tell me that you prowled Martin's house!"

"His desk was right there in the living room!" Pat protested. "I had to go by it on my way to the bathroom. And on my way out I had to go by it again. So I just happened to glance at it, curious."

Barrett glanced away, with a flicker of a smile on his face. "I had a little talk with your husband about curiosity."

155

"What?"

"Nothing. Go ahead."

"I just glanced at Ross' desk and, out of all the papers on it, one caught my eye. It was a note with the word 'guru' that sort of jumped up at me. It stuck in my head and I wrote it down, exactly the way I saw it. It was just the unusual word that got my attention. Those initials didn't mean anything to me until . . ."

"Hold it, Mrs. Pratt!" Barrett cut in. "You were there on the beach! You knew that 'CC' could mean Carl Conley!"

Pat held up her left hand, shaking her head. "No, sir! I was not there when you identified the body. I never heard Carl Conley's name until you and Tony and I were at the cabin."

Barrett rocked his chair back and squinted at the ceiling, thinking. "Right," he said, almost to himself. "You were headed for Martin's house when we identified Conley." He rocked forward and said it again. "You're right."

Pat's head bobbed emphatically. "Of course," she said.

She sat back and let Barrett savor that for a moment before she picked up her thought. "So, as I said, the initials 'CC' didn't mean anything to me."

"But they meant something to you later on that night, when I came to your house to wrap up my report. *Then* you knew it was Carl Conley's body on the beach. *Then* the 'CC' meant something to you. But you still didn't say anything. Why not?"

Pat sounded subdued. "I don't know . . ."

Barrett made a sour face. "'I don't know' again?"

"Yes." She was quiet but emphatic. "I—don't—know why I didn't say anything about the note. Maybe I felt like Tony, my husband—wanting to see if I could figure something out." She shrugged. "I don't know—maybe I thought I would look foolish for writing it down. But at the same time, I *know* that the only thing that caught my attention was the word 'guru.' It's the only thing that struck me as odd. But later, I realized there was something else funny about it."

Holding Pat's copy of the note again Barrett read, "'Guru says OK!' What's funny about that?"

"I'll show you. But first, you tell me how long Martin Ross and Carl Conley had worked together," Pat said, and then she jumped as Barrett's flat hand slapped his desk and he tossed his head back and barked "Ha!"

"Was that meant to be a laugh?"

Barrett smiled. "Martin Ross thought Carl Conley was the phoniest so-and-so this side of the Capitol building in Salem. Told him so, too! 'Carl,' he'd say, 'if you'd stop play-acting all the time you'd be a lot better off. If you'd stop tryin' to be such a big-shot,' he'd say, 'you might even wrap up one of those real estate deals you're always dreaming up.'" Barrett shrugged, and another small smile moved his mustache. "Oh, Martin would cooperate on civic things like the Sand Castle Contest and fixin' up Main Street. But more than that? No, ma'am. No way could they work together!"

Shifting in his chair again, the officer had another

thought. "As a matter of fact, though, Martin's been acting that way with just about everybody in town. Kind of tense and edgy, you know? And nosey." Barrett shook his head. "Even asked me if I knew when your husband was coming back."

Pat's eyes snapped to attention. "So *that's* how he knew."

"What?"

"Nothing. Go ahead."

"Well, I was sayin' that Martin's been acting kind of tense, lately. Edgy, you know? Almost suspicious, you might say."

"'Proprietary'—that's how Maggie described him at the bookstore. 'Acts like he owns Musket Beach,' she said."

Nodding agreement, Barrett added, "Right. And he's afraid somebody's trying to take it away from him."

"Or afraid somebody's going to find out something?"

"What's that supposed to mean?"

"I don't know . . ."

Barrett's face turned sour again. "Another 'I don't know'?"

"Well." Pat shrugged and looked around the little room with an expression that said, "You're not gonna believe this." Finally, she looked Barrett straight in the eye. "Maybe Martin Ross' got something going on with Carole Conley."

Barrett stared. "Ha!"

"Stranger things have happened."

"I can't imagine one. Ha!"

Pat scooted forward on her chair and picked up the note she'd brought in. "Let it pass," she said, changing the subject. "Anyway—" she turned the note so that Barrett could read it and put her finger at the end of the single sentence—"now I'll tell you what's odd about this little message. See that exclamation point?"

"Sure."

"That's what's odd. If that were a simple period, you'd have a simple statement. 'Guru says OK.' A fact. Nothing more. But that exclamation point changes it, makes it important, turns it into some kind of announcement. It makes me think that Ross and 'CC' had been working together on something, whether anybody else knew it or not. And what this note says is, 'We did it! We got what we wanted!'"

Barrett shook his head, looking down at the note. "You're sure hangin' a lot on that little-bitty punctuation mark."

"Bang-mark."

"What?"

"My husband says that sometimes an exclamation point is called a bang-mark. That's what made me think hard about this note: 'Guru says OK! Bang!' Makes it really important."

Barrett stared at the note for several seconds. His eyes narrowed, and a frown made a deep crease between his eyes before he said, "Martin Ross? Conniving with Carl Conley? And *Carole* Conley? And that baby-blue guru and his gang?" He sat straight up,

159

looking hard at Pat and shaking his head. "I'll swear that Ross wasn't hooked up with either *one* of the Conleys. In *anything!*"

Pat stood. "Well, that's not the way I read that bang-mark. But it's up to you, of course."

"Right," Barrett said, squeaking to his feet.

"I just wish you'd think about it. Maybe look around. Try to find out if they *were* working together on something."

"We'll see," he said. "Anyway, thanks for telling me about that metal block. I'll go ahead and call the State Police about it." He put out a large right hand. "And really," he added, "don't worry any more about Martin Ross being mixed up in anything funny."

Pat gave him another shrug and a little sideways look, but she shook his hand before she pushed open the small wooden gate and walked out of his office. Above the racket of the gate swinging shut she heard him call, "If I were you, I'd worry about the tourists, instead. They're gettin' pretty thick out there."

She looked back at him over her shoulder and smiled. "These Sand Castle crowds can be murder, can't they?"

CHAPTER

NINETEEN

Friday Afternoon—
Hollywood to Musket Beach

TONY's jet from Burbank to Portland was a three-holer. Buckling himself into his left-side window seat near the back, he nodded approval. This meant that the Boeing 727 not only had three engines clustered at the tail, it also had a passenger stairway tucked underneath. This, in turn, meant that the crew would probably lower the back stairway for unloading at Portland International, allowing him to get out, down, and through the airport parking lot without going through that long, slow jetway shuffle to the concourse and the main terminal.

He had to get off the plane, fast. Out of the airport, fast. Across almost half of Oregon, fast. But he wasn't sure why. He had to beat Paul Taylor to Musket Beach, but he wasn't sure why. He was sure of only one thing:

161

worry had been chewing at him ever since he'd learned that Taylor had canceled a very important recording date in order to fly back to Musket Beach.

He knew that he had to get to Pat as quickly as possible. But he didn't know why. The one thing he was sure of was the feeling he had. He could feel her calling him. And right now there was nothing he could do about it except ride.

Trying to get his mind on something else, Tony thought back to the recording job he'd left in Hollywood and, when the seat belt sign went off, he pulled the tray-table down, got out his notebook, and drafted a memorandum to Gary Bonham at the advertising agency. He apologized for rushing away, adding—in the kind of sincere, secret, nonspecific language that Bonham loved—"I can only cite urgent, personal reasons." He assured Bonham that Abe and Jax would do an excellent job of finishing the commercials because they knew and understood exactly what Tony wanted. And he cut his fee because he hadn't put in his estimated number of hours.

He wrote a similar memo to Marion Wallingford, just to let The Client know that cutting the fee was Tony's idea.

He made a note to send copies of the memos to Abe and Jax, for their own amusement.

Finished with his writing, Tony looked out the window and let worry start chewing again. Somewhere far away to his left, and far below those clouds spread out like a dimpled white comforter, Paul Taylor was probably racing his own plane—a twin-tailed Bell Aeronca, Rolly had said—toward the same goal that Tony had. But when Taylor landed at Seashore Airport on the coast, he'd be more than ninety miles closer to Pat than Tony. And though the jet was three-hundred-miles-an-hour faster than Taylor's plane, Taylor had more than a two-hour head start. And Martin Ross was already there.

Shortly after five o'clock, the 727 approached Portland International Airport through low clouds and landed in a misty wind. Despite the damp, the crew lowered the back stairs and Tony bounded down. He rushed across the tarmac and into the terminal, up the ramp and down the concourse, where the clocks all said five-thirty, more or less.

Taylor's plane was probably still in the air somewhere along the Oregon coast, nose pointed at Seashore.

At a bank of telephones near the rental car desks, Tony stopped for a minute to call the cabin again. Still no Pat. He hurried out and across the wet, windy parking lot, climbed into his Capri, and headed for Musket Beach, almost a hundred miles away.

An hour and fifty minutes later Tony turned left off Oregon Highway 26 and drove south on U.S. 101 as it curled around the flank of Mount Kenai. He was pleased at the time he'd made in the Fourth of July Weekend traffic, but surprised that a bank of fog was rolling in and rapidly turning the coastline dark.

He passed by the first exit leading to the long, narrow town perched above the Pacific shore and turned right at the second. This access road doubled back in the direction he'd come, but after two short blocks he made a left turn toward the ocean and drove slowly down the pocked gravel road that passed in front of the cabin. The fog and the darkness were getting thicker, as though the sun had disappeared, but there was still almost an hour until sunset.

Of the seven houses on the road, only two showed any hint of light. At the end of the road, a faint corona of watery pink glowed around the lone street lamp.

Tony turned the headlights on and leaned forward, pressing against the steering wheel, looking hard but seeing little. His headlights bored into the blowing, drifting fog and glanced off the wet windows and chrome trim of their Volvo parked beside the cabin. Pat was here!

Tony took a deep breath. Sitting back a little from the steering wheel, he gave the horn his usual three quick taps.

But the cabin was dark. There was no light gleaming through the blinds, no smoke rising from the chimney. As he swung in to park beside the Volvo his headlights swept along the length of the cabin and flashed across the startled white face and gleaming wet poncho of somebody on the back deck.

Before Tony could stop the car and fix him in the

headlights, the figure whirled away toward the back fence and vanished in the dark and the fog.

Tony braked and lunged for the flashlight in the glove box.

Lights came on inside the cabin.

He scrambled out of the car and around to the steps.

A dog barked loud and hard beyond the fence.

The light on the front deck suddenly blossomed in the fog.

Tony ran up the steps and across the deck. The front door opened. A spray of light washed across the deck and then Pat was in the doorway, eyes wide, face tense and pale, hair mussed. She reached out to him, saying softly, "You're back! You're back!"

"Yes," he said, taking her, holding her, his voice a rough whisper. "I'm here. But what's wrong?—why've you been in there with the lights out?"

She wrapped her arms tight around his waist. "I heard a noise. On the back deck. I was afraid someone might be peeking in, like before. So I turned the lights off."

"Did you call Barrett?"

"Yes. I got that stupid answering machine."

She burrowed her head into his shoulder and under his chin, squeezing her eyes shut, forcing tears out the corners. "You're back."

They held each other close, in the fog, and he only jumped a little when she dropped the poker by his right foot.

TWENTY

Friday Night— The Cabin

MUCH later, inside the small cabin, lights glowed warm and bright. A crackling fire worked its wonders in the wood stove, and a Martha's Company Casserole was baking in the oven.

"Feeling better?"

Tony asked his question to the top of Pat's head as they nestled together on the couch.

He had checked all around the outside of the fog-bound cabin, inspecting every inch in the harsh glare of his big emergency flashlight. With Pat alongside in her yellow slicker—she had firmly refused to stay in the cabin alone—Tony'd been especially thorough covering the back deck and yard, including the wood pile. The only thing he'd found that might be considered unusual was a bootprint in the mud near an opening in the rickety back fence.

By putting a couple of pieces of firewood along each side of it, Tony had marked the print to make it easier to find when Officer Barrett arrived later—Pat's telephone call to police headquarters about the prowler having brought a tape-recorded promise that "the duty officer will get back to you as soon as possible."

Then, their inspection finished, they'd come back inside and sat knee-to-knee at the kitchen divider, discussing things over Old-Fashioned glasses of J&B Scotch with a dollop of water.

Pat told Tony about nosy Martin Ross and how he always seemed to be around: in the bank, at the bookstore, walking past the cabin every day, even showing up at Taylor's house. She told him about Taylor's place, about its beautiful setting and all the land around it, and his recording studio and the tape machine with the scuffed spot on top. She told him about tearing into Martin Ross, and about going to see Officer Barrett, and about showing Barrett "the guru note."

Tony heard most of it, but he kept getting mad at Ross for frightening Pat. Twice he tried to call the grocer to unload on him, but each time he got a busy signal.

Then Tony told Pat about his introduction to Carole Conley—"Carole with an 'e'," he remembered—and about how much younger she was than her late husband. Tony described how Carole seemed to be unaware that she was a widow, and he wondered, again, how Paul Taylor had come to know Pat's name.

And the more he thought about that, the more convinced he became that he should call Taylor and ask to see his studio; maybe then he could find out how the actor knew about Pat. Again he got a busy signal.

Tony put the phone down and looked at Pat. There was an odd smile on his face. "Wouldn't it be funny if Martin Ross and Paul Taylor were talking to each other?"

Her eyebrows pulled together in a frown. "I don't know. I'm not so sure about that."

Tony had started to pour another Scotch, then changed his mind. With Officer Barrett coming over, he'd said, perhaps tea would be a smarter move.

So they were now on the couch, wound as closely and as intricately as possible without spilling their mugs of Chinese Green. The kitchen timer ticked away over the casserole like a watchful friend.

"Yes," Pat said. "Much better. But I'm sorry that you rushed away from the job in L.A. just because your wife didn't answer the phone."

"There's more to it than that, you know. And I still don't know where you were."

Leaning her shoulders away slightly, Pat looked up at Tony. "I thought I told you."

"No."

169

She sipped a sip of tea. "Told you everything else, how could I miss that?"

He shrugged. "Don't know."

"The memory is going. Fast." After a sad wave of her head she resettled it on his shoulder and, with a rising inflection as though continuing an unfinished story, she said, "Okaaay. After I went to the police station and talked with Officer Barrett this morning—around noon would be more like it, I guess—I went shopping and ran into Betty Meadows. So we had lunch at The Crab Pot and talked for quite a while and . . ."

"It must have been a good l-o-o-ng while."

"Well, I was pretty wound up, you know, after my little donnybrook with Martin Ross. And then my talk with Barrett. So I guess I had a lot to say. And then *Betty* had a lot to talk about because . . ."

"All afternoon?"

"Most of it." Pat squirmed a bit. "Then she asked me to go along while she looked at a house that she and Bill are thinking of buying, and I found out something very interesting. She said that . . ."

"I thought Bill and Betty already owned that house down the street."

Pat shifted again. In the process, she leaned back and focused a quick look on Tony, her left eyebrow raised. Then she went on. "No, they lease that place." She paused. "Which reminds me: We're going there tomorrow for their annual Fourth of July party."

This time Tony looked embarrassed. "Oh-oh."

"Just as I thought," she said quietly before going on, "It's more of a potluck, really. Very casual. Sort of a whoever's-in-the-neighborhood-drop-in-and-bring-some-eats thing."

She reached across Tony to put her tea cup on the coffee table. "Anyway! They're looking for a house, as I was saying. And she's working through one of the local realtors, and that real estate lady has stuffed Betty with all kinds of local gossip about ..."

Tony eased away from Pat and sat up. "I'd better put some more wood on the fire."

When he interrupted, Pat stopped talking but her mouth stayed open. She pushed herself up and closed her mouth. Watching Tony, a slight frown drew a thin crease between her eyes. She leaned back on the couch and stretched out, ankles crossed on the coffee table.

Sitting on the edge of the coffee table, Tony slid a few inches along it to the front of the wood stove while he asked, "Did you happen to ask Betty if she ever worked with a real estate man named Carl Conley?"

Pat looked hard at the back of his head before she said, with firm emphasis on the negatives, "Yes, I did, and no, she didn't, and yes, she heard something about him but no, I won't tell you if you keep interrupting me like this."

Tony twisted around and looked at his wife for a couple of seconds, surprised. Turning back to the stove, he opened its door and worked a large piece of alder into the flames. Closing the door, he turned again to Pat, solemnly brushing his fingers together like the fastidious Oliver Hardy. He cupped his hands in his lap, sitting still and attentive.

"Very good." Pat picked up her cup and sipped

another sip before going on rapidly. "No, Betty never had any dealings with Carl Conley but she knew the name. But her point was that her real estate broker was pretty free with her conversation and pretty derogatory about her competitors, *especially* Carl Conley." Pat paused, looking at Tony. "You're not saying anything."

Tony's head wagged.

She nodded her approval. "Good dog," she said quietly. Then she went on with her story, getting more and more involved in it. "According to what Betty Meadows heard, the hottest gossip in Musket Beach is about real estate. Her broker says there's a new real estate rumor running around town almost every day. 'A really big deal is coming through,' they say. 'It's so big that Musket Beach is gonna double in size.' 'There'll be so much money around town, we'll all be swimming in it.'"

Pat paused a moment, calming. "The sad part of it is, Carl Conley seems to be a part of it. Even though he's dead. And people seem to be laughing about him. 'Sounds like one of his deals,' they say." She stopped, stretching her neck and head back, squinting at the ceiling. "What is it they say? 'He's got nothin' to sell, but he sells it like hell.' And they laugh."

She shuddered, looking down into her cup, squeezing it in the circle of her hands.

Tony moved back to the couch and sat beside her, putting an arm around her shoulders.

"Anyway," she went on, "Betty says that *commercial* property in Musket Beach is just frozen. Nobody selling, nobody buying." She looked at Tony. "Really strange, isn't it? From everything that we've seen and heard, this has always been a very active real estate market. Now, all of a sudden: nothing. It's as though people were standing around waiting for something to happen." Pat looked away, shaking her head in wonder. "But at the same time, *residential* prices are going crazy. Insane! Higher than ever!"

Tony opened his mouth to speak but at that moment, outside the cabin, a car door slammed and heavy footsteps thumped quickly up the steps and across the front deck. He jumped to his feet and hurried around the end of the couch, getting to the door just as it shivered under a hard pound, pound, pound.

He pulled aside the curtain covering the small window and looked into Officer Barrett's pale face, wet and worried in the fog. The moisture in his hair and on his forehead and along the tops of his eyebrows glistened in the overhead porch light. His mustache and his lower jaw seemed lost in deep shadow.

Tony unlocked the door and pulled it open. Barrett stood there, swiveling his head around, right and left, squinting into the fog. "Everybody okay?" he asked loudly, now looking down over the edge of the deck.

"Fine, sure, everybody's fine!" Tony called back, standing beside the open door. "And thanks for coming." He gestured to Pat on his way to the kitchen counter to pick up his flashlight. "And say hello again to my wife, since this is the second time you've seen her today."

"Sure is. Hi again, Mrs. Pratt."

Pat smiled. "Barry."

"What's this about a prowler?"

Pat told him about hearing a noise on the back deck and calling the police to report. Tony described the way his headlights flashed over a face and a slicker as he drove up to the cabin. And they both talked about searching the grounds as Tony opened the door again, leading Pat and Barrett outside. "Let's go around the place again," he said, "and we'll show you what we found in back."

"And that was?"

"A footprint. A bootprint."

They went slowly around the cabin, flashlight beams jabbing in and around the big sword-leaf ferns and wild blackberry, the escallonia and salal. They crossed and recrossed the back yard, working their way toward the pine trees and the woodpile. Finally they reached the fence and stood over the spot where Tony had marked the bootprint with two pieces of firewood. Both pieces were there, but the end of one piece was black and muddy. The bootprint was scratched out.

TWENTY·ONE

Friday Night—
The Cabin, Musket Beach
(continued)

In the cabin, still wearing her yellow slicker, Pat stood behind the counter separating the kitchen from the living room and emptied a can of root beer into a glass. She slid the fizzing glass across to the other side of the counter where Officer Barrett and Tony sat. The policeman gave her a quick look and nod of thanks while he rubbed a big red bandana over his head, sopping up the moisture glinting in his hair. They'd all been outside in the fog again, this time to have Pat point out the first bootprint, the one she'd found near the back deck on the night that Martin Ross had loomed up, eerie and frightening, behind the woodpile.

Tony, like Barrett, sat slumped over, elbows on the counter. He stared at his hands as he slowly rubbed his palms together.

After pouring a cup of tea for herself, Pat held up the teapot for Tony to see. He glanced at it, shook his head, and went back to staring at his hands.

She put the pot back on the stove before looking at each of them and asking, "So, what do you think?— would the bootprint *I* found match the one you saw by the fence tonight?"

"I don't know," Tony sighed. "I *think* they were the same size. But what do I know from footprints?"

Barrett gazed tiredly from husband to wife. "It's possible they were *both* made at the same time, you know." He picked up his root beer, but before taking a sip he said to Pat, "The one by the fence could've been made at the same time as the one you saw last night. Or the night before, whenever you were out back."

"Last night." She stared down into her cup of tea, shaking her head slowly. "Seems longer. Seems like a week."

"Listen . . ." Tony started to say, and just then the kitchen timer gave a long, loud ring over the casserole.

Pat checked her watch quickly before prompting Tony. "Go ahead," she told him. "I'll give it a couple of minutes more before I turn the oven off."

"What I was going to say is," Tony continued, "all this stuff that's going on around here must have something to do with Conley. With Conley's body, I mean."

His voice was quiet but emphatic, his eyes serious as he looked from Barrett to Pat and back to Barrett. "We never had people prowling around this place before. Not until we found that body. Pat never had Martin Ross showing up at the store and the bank and coming by here at all hours. And: Never before have I gone down to Hollywood and met an actor who knows my wife's name."

Tony's eyes fixed on the officer's. The fingers of his right hand, bunched together, tapped on the countertop. "Finding the body. That has to be the thing that started all of this. So what I want to know is," and here he held his hand out toward Barrett, "what kind of connection is there between Conley, Ross, and Taylor?"

Barrett's voice was equally quiet and emphatic. "That's what I want to know, too, Mr. Pratt. Among other things. And it just happens to be my line of work. Not yours." The policeman looked at Pat. "And not yours, either, ma'am."

"Now wait a minute." Tension began creeping into Tony's voice. "It's *my* wife who is being followed around, it's *our* house that's being watched, and it's . . ."

Barrett interrupted, turning on the stool to face Tony, strain beginning to edge into his voice, too. "And it's *my* job to find out who's doing it. You may be good at playing cop in your stories, but *being* a cop is very much different from writing about it."

Pat looked quickly from Barrett to Tony and back again and tried to head off any further confrontation. "We understand that," she said. "And we appreciate it. But there's just you and one other officer."

"I'll get what help I need when I need it," Barrett said patiently.

He started to rise, but instead turned back to the counter and picked up his root beer. "I've talked to the county sheriff and he's sending some people over here, anyway, because of the Fourth of July. Musket Beach always draws big crowds on holidays, so if we need extra officers, we got 'em. And I got word from Oregon State Police Headquarters in Salem that a couple of state troopers will be here tomorrow."

Barrett raised his glass but before he could drink Tony cut in sharply.

"Tomorrow! But somebody's been prowling around here *tonight!*"

"We'll keep an eye out." Barrett took two long swallows of root beer.

Pat put her teacup on the counter. "I thought you were off duty?"

Rubbing a forefinger across his mustache, Barrett started to get up again. "We'll do what we have to do."

Tony persisted. "Okay, just tell me one thing: Do *you* see any connection between those three? Between Ross and Conley and Taylor?"

Barrett eased back down onto the stool and Pat reminded him of his strong opinions earlier in the day. "When I was in your office," she said, "you told me that Ross wouldn't have anything to do with Conley."

"And as far as I know, that's true." There was a furrow between Barrett's dark brows and he stroked his mustache again. "I don't know of any 'connection' at all between Ross and Conley—no indication that they were working together on *anything*. And I don't know

178

about anything going on between Ross and Taylor, either.

"As for the other—Taylor and Conley? Could be. Maybe some real estate deal or something." Barrett stopped and chuckled. "But if Taylor was gonna sell his property, I really don't believe he was planning to do it through Carl Conley."

Startled, Pat and Tony looked at each other and together they almost shouted, "What?"

"So *that's* it!" Pat went on. "*That's* the big real estate deal I've been hearing all the rumors about!"

Barrett shook his head and blinked, surprised at their reactions. "But I thought that's what you were getting at!—the story goin' around that Taylor hired Conley to sell his property—the house and all that land behind it?"

It was Tony's turn to shake his head, trying to keep up as Pat rushed on, "That's all we've heard, rumors. But nothing specific. Just that some big deal was in the works, something worth umpty-ump millions. But we never heard any names mentioned."

"Truth is," Barrett went on, "I don't think Taylor'd sell that land, anyway. As I understand it, that's why he bought the property in the first place: For the privacy."

He gave a quick, soundless laugh that made his broad shoulders shrug a couple of times. "And, also from what I've heard about him, I 'specially don't think he'd want a bunch of religious fanatics for neighbors."

"How do you mean?"

"Well, one of the *other* rumors is that that religious

outfit wants to buy Taylor's land—that bunch that marched through town in blue suits and Rolls Royces." He raised his glass and drained the little bit of root beer. He wiped the foam off his mustache with a finger and gave a little belch, as if dismissing baby-blue costumes and shiny Rolls Royces. "They're looking to build a settlement or something on it—a whatchamacallit. Commune! But, like I said, I don't think Taylor'd sell to those folks."

Barrett's belly bounced with one of his short, barking laughs. "And, since Taylor was messin' around with *Carole* Conley, I really don't think he'd try to work out a real estate deal with *Carl!*"

Pat turned slowly to Tony, Tony turned slowly to Pat, then they both turned to Barrett, who was grinning into his empty glass. After a couple of seconds he felt the Pratts staring at him and his grin disappeared.

Tony watched Barrett but nodded toward Pat. "Remember the note that Pat saw on Martin Ross' desk?"

She leaned forward, looking at the policeman. "I showed you a copy of that note in your office, remember? 'Martin, Guru says okay, bang!' Remember that?"

Barrett's mouth opened and closed and opened again. "Well, I'll be damned." Looking down, he wagged his head slowly from side to side. "And I thought I knew all there was to know about Musket Beach."

They were all quiet, and then Tony spoke to Barrett, but his eyes were on Pat. "Here's something else to think about. That note was signed 'CC,' but—" Pat's eyebrows rose and she nodded at Tony—"what if 'CC' should turn out to be *Carole* Conley?"

Barrett couldn't believe it. "CarolMae?"

Pat nodded again. "As I said, 'Stranger things have happened.'"

Tony looked from one to the other. "Maybe Carol-Mae thought she'd finally found a way to strike it rich in Musket Beach."

"Well," Barrett said. "I'll be damned. Martin Ross and CarolMae. Wouldn't that be a pair to draw to?"

They sat there for several seconds, in silent thought. And then all three sniffed and jumped up and looked at the stove. "Aarrgh!" Pat growled. "Aargh! Aargh! Aargh!" Rushing across the kitchen, she yanked open the oven door and crouched down in a cloud of thick, dark smoke, waving her potholder sadly over the black top of her Martha's Company Casserole.

TWENTY-TWO

Saturday Morning—
The Cabin, Musket Beach

By Saturday morning, the smell of burnt noodles and cheese was almost gone from the cabin. Or, more likely, it was merely masked by the scent of wood smoke from the stove and by the remaining faint aroma of The Pizza Parlor's sausage-and-anchovy special which Pat and Tony had called in to replace the Martha's Company Casserole. In either case, when the Pratts came down for breakfast they noticed nothing in the air to remind them that last night's dinner had gone up in smoke.

And, despite Friday evening's upsets, Tony and Pat looked fresh and rested. They seemed to have slept well and soundly, completely unaware of the deep, rumbling engine and crunching tires of the Musket Beach police car as it rolled back and forth on the gravel road in front of the cabin at irregular intervals during the night, or of the piercing beam of the spotlight that poked now and then at the fog around the cabin.

Fixing breakfast, Pat washed a big handful of Oregon's famous Hood strawberries and sliced them on bowls of Wheat Chex cereal. Tony made coffee and ran the toaster.

After breakfast they washed and dried the dishes, each carefully ignoring the blackened casserole dish soaking in the sink. Then they carried their coffee mugs to the front deck to savor the morning.

Tony looked eastward, to his right, where the foothills of the Coast Range rose a few miles away, then he looked straight up, and then to the left toward the ocean.

Bright, warm sunshine was clearing last night's fog off the hilltops to the east, leaving just a scattering of gray-white fingers and tendrils reaching low into the deep green forest ridges. Overhead, blue sky beamed through a thinning gauze of mist.

Giving way before the sunlight, the fog held on most persistently over the sea, where it hung in drifting gray scrims swinging above the rolling white surf line.

Turning his back to the sun, Tony watched the half-hidden surf break white and gray beneath the fog. "Seems to be burning off."

"Good." Pat put her coffee mug beside his on the flat two-by-eight top railing that ran around the deck. Hoisting herself up, she sat on the rail and spun around to face the ocean. She rested her heels on the middle rail, picked up her mug, and stretched her shoulders forward like a cat to catch the sun. "Feels nice on the back."

He nodded and said quickly, "Great day for the Sand Castle Contest. How do you feel about walking up the beach to take a look?"

Her eyes went suddenly blank over the rim of her coffee cup. "You're very cheery. But are you serious?"

"Sure. The walk would probably do us good."

Pat looked at him, squinting a little. Her voice a bit grim. "Don't you want to talk about it any more? This Conley-Taylor-Ross connection?"

He picked up his coffee cup and sipped, frowning, before he leaned back against the door frame. "Don't you think we came close to talking it to death last night? And we don't know any more now than we did then. All that we have, still, are some rumors and a note."

"And a body," she reminded him.

He paused. "True."

"And somebody prowling around the place," she added.

"Also true," he agreed soberly, "which makes me even more inclined to go along with Barrett and let the officers of the law 'do their thing,' as the saying goes."

Pat thought for a moment. "You're probably right." She nodded, then looked at him with a quick, wry glance. "They certainly 'did their thing' last night!"

"You mean those patrols past the house?" Tony

185

smiled a little, too, and leaned down, elbows and forearms resting on the rail beside his wife. "I thought you were asleep and didn't hear it."

"A couple of times. Maybe it was the light." She looked sideways at him. "I thought you were asleep, too."

"Probably was," he smiled again, "most of the time." He pushed himself away from the railing and stood up, putting his right hand lightly on her warm back. His fingers massaged gently between her shoulder blades and he asked in a brighter tone, "Anyway, what do you think: Shall we take a walk and see the sand castles?"

After a moment, Pat sat up and her face lightened and she shrugged her left shoulder. "Why not?" she said, as she raised her knees high, spun around on the railing, and hopped down to the deck alongside Tony. Turning to face the ocean, she started to wrap her arm around his waist but suddenly said, "Oh-oh" and began to wave, instead.

"What's 'oh-oh'?" Tony asked. He looked to see what she was waving at. About fifty yards away, standing by the flagpole in the side yard of their house on the bank overlooking the beach, Bill and Betty Meadows waved back as they prepared to hoist a big American flag. Tony tossed a salute in their direction, at the same time saying to Pat, "I repeat, why do you say 'Oh-oh'?"

"Seeing Betty over there reminded me of her party."

"Oh-ho!"

"You forgot it, too, didn't you?"

"What time?"

"Noonish. And we won't have to stay long. We can just stop in for a few minutes, have a little bite, and then go on to see the sand castles."

"Can't be *too* long or the tide'll wash 'em away before we get there."

"Now all I have to do is think of something to take," Pat said, heading into the cabin.

Tony leaned back against the railing, saying loudly, "I have a suggestion!"

"Which is?"

"Fruit salad. Easy, quick, and I can help."

"Good idea!"

Out of the kitchen came noises—the refrigerator door opening; the rattle and clank of bottles and jars being pushed around; drawers being pulled open and shoved shut; the word "Rats!" And a solid thunk as the refrigerator door slammed shut.

Pat appeared in the doorway holding a peach in the palm of her hand. "One peach."

"Not much."

"But I'm not in the mood for Martin Ross *or* his grocery store!"

"Understandable. So why don't we get the bikes out and ride up to Cappy's?"

So instead of driving two miles to Ross' Musket Beach Market, they peddled their rusty old three-speed bikes to the little mom-and-pop grocery on the highway, about half-way to town.

After that, they gave the rest of the morning to

peeling, paring, slicing, and chopping. They spooned the fruit salad into the big wooden bowl and Tony carried it as they walked down the gravel road to the Meadows' Fourth of July potluck precisely at Pat's appointed hour—noonish.

It was, as she'd predicted, a casual and free-flowing affair. People showed up when they felt like it, most of them bringing a pan, platter, plastic bowl, or paper plate wrapped in aluminum foil. The food was spread out on a long trestle table, on one end of which sat a big red-and-white Coleman cooler filled with ice, soft drinks and champagne.

"Huh!" Tony grunted, pointing with a carrot stick at the cups and glasses by the cooler. "A touch of class: paper cups for the soft drinks but real glasses for the champagne."

"Betty's a true believer," Pat said, picking up a slice of jicama. "In her opinion, you can't hurt a Coke or Pepsi, no matter *what* you drink it out of. But she thinks it's near sacrilege to drink champagne out of plastic. 'Champagne deserves real glass,' she says."

"Sensible woman," Tony said, reaching for one of the chilled green bottles. "Ready for some?"

"One. Let's have one while we nibble and mill, and then we'll walk on up the beach to see the sand castles."

Tony filled two glasses and handed one to Pat. After sipping a toast to each other, they went their separate ways—"milling," as they put it—wandering through the growing crowd, nodding and chatting with the people whose faces they'd come to know during the year or so that they'd owned the beach cabin.

After several minutes, Tony moved around to the side yard and into a game of horseshoes with a retired judge, an attorney, and a high school physics teacher.

Pat, in the midst of more real estate stories from Betty Meadows, found herself being stared at by a tall, milky-eyed man who was turning gray at the temples and round at the middle. Before Pat could stop her, Betty excused herself to greet some new guests. The man stepped into the place where she'd been standing, directly in front of Pat.

"That's really your name?" he asked. "Pat? Pat Pratt?"

Immediately, Pat knew his next moves: the sly look out of the corner of his eye; the voice like a soft, slow purr; the gesture with his hand. And she knew the words. As if on cue, he moved his right hand insinuatingly toward her hip and said, "And may I pat, Pratt?"

Pat sipped her champagne, looking into his eyes over the rim of her glass. When she lowered the glass she lowered her lashes and let her eyes smile. She licked the tip of her tongue along her lip. She waved the glittering, brittle glass slowly under his nose. Still smiling, she murmured, "Do so, and you will become, instantly, the world's oldest boy soprano."

The man's milky blue eyes popped open and his mouth popped shut. At that moment, Tony appeared by Pat's elbow asking, "And who is this?"

In answer, she asked him another question. "Since we've been married, how many times have we heard the 'pat Pratt' line?"

"About five hundred."

She cocked her head at the still-staring man. "Meet Mr. Five-Hundred-And-One."

Tony nodded, "How do you do, Mr. One. Funny, you don't *look* Oriental."

Pat took Tony's arm, hugging it close and leading him away as she murmured, "As for you, good-lookin', how would you like to come up to my place and see some nice sand castles."

After walking around the low hedge of escallonia separating the Meadows' side yard from the path to the beach, Tony and Pat stood on the bank above the sand and enjoyed the view. It was a glorious sunshining day. The fog had burned away leaving behind a beautiful blue sky, cloudless except for the fat cumulus resting on the horizon line perhaps twenty miles out to sea. The ocean reflected the sky in deepening shades till the blue was nearly black at the horizon. Closer, the surf blossomed blue-green and white. Above the beach, bright-colored kites were bobbing and swooping in the holiday sunlight.

Climbing down to the beach brought a change in perspective that brought a change in colors; now the rolling combers were all foamy white, the sea a steady sky-blue. Tony and Pat turned north, with the ocean to their left. Straight ahead stood the green-sided slopes of Mount Kenai, four-thousand feet tall, with the town tucked against its southern side.

Here, at low tide, the beach was about one-hundred-fifty yards wide, sloping gradually up to a seawall of basalt boulders. Along the seawall, smoke rising from charcoal fires in a couple of small Weber barbecues and three or four hibachis drifted up through a yellow metal lifeguard tower. Above the seawall, clustered behind a row of stunted pines, rose the weathered silver siding of some of the first homes in Musket Beach. Farther along, the seawall ended and a blacktop access road came down to the sand. Just past this break in the wall hunkered the wide, flat Sun-Surf Motel & Coffee Shoppe. Beyond the motel, the sand drifted on north into dunes that leaned against a high, fir-topped slope of Mount Kenai.

By the time Tony and Pat reached Musket Beach, the tide was past its low and beginning to rise again. Their approach took them around the southern end of a section of beach set aside for the Sand Castle Contest. A stretch of sand half as wide and fully as long as a football field, it was now carved into three parallel rows of sand sculptures.

Clots of people, loose and colorful in their at-the-beach costumes, shuffled through the sand, leaving the contest site, knowing that the tide had turned and would soon wash over the first row of sculptures. A few people, however, stayed on, wandering casually around and through the fifteen-foot-square plots, now that the stake-and-rope lanes had been taken down. A few others, mostly children, went down to the widening strand of wet sand to wade in the water.

By the top row of sculptures stood the tired, happy

people who had run the contest, measured the plots, manned food booths, brought in portable johns: members of the Musket Beach Volunteer Fire Department in bright red nylon windbreakers, their wives or otherwise, members of the Chamber of Commerce, and other locals. Beer cans in hand, they talked and laughed under clouds of sharp-smelling smoke from their odd-looking cigarettes.

Tony and Pat strolled among the giant sculptures, commenting on some that they especially liked. Here was a huge Darth Vader mask; there was Snoopy in helmet and goggles flying his Sopwith Camel, with Woodstock in the front cockpit. And here Rapunzel leaned from the tower of a seven-tiered castle, hair trailing down to the moat around the base.

Donald Duck marched by in his University of Oregon letter sweater, leading Hughie, Dewey, and Louie. Goofy played baseball in the sand. Snow White hopped into bed with Happy, Dopey, and Doc.

Pat was pointing this one out to Tony when shrill, soaring screams ripped across the beach. Everyone froze for half a second. Then they all turned, searching, till their wide eyes focused on two teen-age girls who were jumping up and down in the rising tide, pointing at something in the first row of sculptures.

Three of the firemen raced toward the girls. Tony and Pat quickly followed. The lifeguard's yellow Jeep sprouted rooster-tails of sand and kicked across the beach. Sirens covered the screams. Running, Pat looked over her shoulder as the brown Musket Beach Police car churned away from the foot of the blacktop access road. Down the road came a white Oregon State Police car, red and blue lights spinning.

A strong wave rolled in past the leaping, screaming girls and onto the mound of sand they pointed to. Their feet pounded the water and splashed wet sand over their brown goose-pimpled legs and white T-shirts. Their screams faded with the dying whine of the sirens and the girls threw their arms around each other and looked away from the mound of eroding sand.

Police car doors slammed as Pat and Tony stopped behind the firemen who crouched around the pile of wet sand. Resting in the sand was a pale, delicate forearm. Pat turned away and ducked her head on Tony's chest. He put his right arm around her shoulders.

One of the firemen, stocky and blond, dropped to one knee and reached for the wrist as a shallow wave ran up the beach, washing away more sand. The forearm now had an elbow. The upper arm disappeared into the mound of sand.

The other two firemen, feet spread wide, stepped carefully closer to the mound and, using the sides of their cupped hands, gently scraped and pulled at the sand over the body. Officer Barrett, bare-headed, and the state trooper in his gray Smokey Bear hat leaned over the kneeling fireman, who dropped the limp wrist and shook his head. The trooper motioned to the sobbing girls to come up the beach and out of the water.

193

Curious people began crowding around. Barrett herded them back, then got into his car and turned it parallel to the beach, bumper-to-bumper with the trooper's car, forming a barricade.

More firemen arrived. Barrett had them line up in their red jackets beside the police cars to keep the crowd away. He told the lifeguard to bring the stretcher from his Jeep just as Tony said, "Good God!"

Pat jerked her head up to look at his face.

Barrett turned quickly, too. "What?" he barked.

"It's Carole Conley!"

Through blinking, narrowed eyes Pat looked past the blond fireman to the mushy sand, to the arm, to the now-exposed left shoulder and chest before she turned back to Tony. Her voice cracked slightly when she asked, "How can you tell?"

"Her shoulder." He spoke rapidly, excited. "The dress strap. She was wearing that same dress when I saw her in Hollywood yesterday. With Paul Taylor!"

He started across the beach, head down, pushing through the crowd beside the cars.

"Tony!" Pat yelled, rushing after him.

Barrett's voice boomed, "Mr. Pratt!"

It was a quiet voice directly in front of him that made Tony stop. "Mr. Pratt, is it?"

Tony's eyes moved up the sharply creased blue trousers to the sharply creased gray shirt front with neatly buttoned pocket flaps and the black name-tag that read "Trooper Kelsey," past the square chin, thin

194

lips, and long nose and into his own reflection doubled in the state trooper's sunglasses.

Trooper Kelsey's thin lips moved just enough to let out his ice-cold voice. "I believe my colleague, Officer Barrett, wants a few words with you."

"Where do you think you're goin', Mr. Pratt?" Barrett was on Tony's left as Pat came up and held his right hand.

"To Taylor's. Taylor's place." Tony sounded nervous, almost panting, compared to Barrett's calm response.

"No, sir. You're going home." The officer was looking down. The wet bottoms of his dark brown uniform pants were as black as his wet black shoes.

"But somebody's got to *do* something about this guy!"

Barrett's voice sounded as hard as the look he gave Tony. "Mr. Pratt, we've covered this subject several times, including last night. This is police work. And something *is* being done. By law enforcement officers." Barrett spoke very methodically. "We're moving that body up away from the tide, we're calling the medical examiner, we're gonna see what else we can find under that pile of sand, and we've got the State Police here." Barrett nodded toward Trooper Kelsey. Then he glowered at Tony and Pat, almost giving orders. "You and Mrs. Pratt go home and stay there, please. Till I come and get your statement. About when and where you saw Carole Conley last. *If* that's Carole Conley." He

195

started to leave but stopped and added quickly, "I'll see you at your place as soon as we're finished here. Please." He went back through the line of bystanders.

Tony squeezed Pat's hand. "Let's go," he said sharply, and started away.

"Where to?"

"You heard the man," he said, his voice rising to make sure that Trooper Kelsey heard. "We're going home!" And then in an undertone, "To get the car."

TWENTY-THREE

Saturday Afternoon—
Taylor's House

PAT slammed the car door, yanked her seat belt around, and clacked the buckle into place. Emphatically, she said, "This is a pretty scary thing to be doing, you know!" She turned half-way around and frowned at Tony as he put the ignition key in. "There are those, in fact, who would call it stupid."

The engine started.

Tony raised his right forefinger. "They also serve who only stand and water the pyracantha," he said, before resting his right hand on her leg. "And if you, my dear, would rather stay and tend the flowers . . ."

"Alone? No, sir! Besides, I'm the only one in this car who knows where Paul Taylor lives." Settling into her seat, she said, "I'm also the only one who doesn't know exactly why we're going there."

The tires spattered gravel as Tony backed the Volvo onto the road and spun the steering wheel to start up the slope to the main road.

"One reason we're going there is this: While the cops are busy on the beach, nobody's keeping an eye on Paul Taylor. Another reason? As I mentioned before, he knew your name when I was introduced to him in Hollywood, even though neither of us had met him. That, it seems to me, is very odd. So, it also seems to me, somebody here in Musket Beach must've told him about us."

"How? And who? And why?"

"By phone. And who?" He shrugged. "There are only two other people connected to the bodies that are falling around here. A grocer and a cop. As for the why . ." His voice trailed off and he shrugged again.

Pat crossed her legs and folded her arms. "Wonderful."

At the corner, instead of turning left toward Musket Beach he turned right on the highway access road. "I remember what Rolly Nidecker said at the recording session about . . ."

Pat interrupted. "Why are we going this way? He lives at the other end of town."

"I don't want to drive through that Sand Castle crowd on Main Street. And I don't want to chance bumping into Officer Barrett just now. So we'll take the highway around and drop down into town at the other end of Main. Didn't you say Taylor lives on Cedar Street?"

198

"Right. On the ocean side of Main."

"Right."

"Okay. Now. You were saying?"

At the stop sign Tony made a left turn and drove north on Highway 101 as he recalled what Rolly Nidecker had told him in Hollywood.

"There were some long distance calls for Taylor during his session, when I was waiting in the office. One of the calls came from here, from Musket Beach. Rolly was steamed, really teed off. 'Jeez, Paul gets calls—even his *girl friend* gets calls!' he said. 'In the middle of a *session!*' So I want to ask Taylor about those phone calls."

And he repeated something that Paul Taylor had told Rolly Nidecker.

"According to Rolly, Taylor said, 'A wife can cause a lot of trouble, especially if she's not your own.' Or words to that effect."

Pat made an unladylike noise.

"Right," Tony agreed. "Rolly laughed when he told me; he thought that Taylor was talking about Carole Conley. And I would have thought so, too, but I'd just tried to call you at the cabin and you weren't there. Now, you're not usually out at that time of day, so I started to worry. I called Barrett at the police department. I wanted him to check on you, but he said that he had seen you at Taylor's place."

Pat started to say something, but Tony raised his right hand from the steering wheel for a second. "At the time, remember, I didn't *know* that Martin Ross was following you all over town; and I didn't know that he was telling Taylor about it."

"Wait a second. How do you know it *now?* And we'd better get in the outside lane; the turn-off's coming up."

"Right. Well, it's a guess. But later—when Taylor said your name—I knew that he had to get it from somebody here in Musket Beach. And there were only two people who could connect us with Carl Conley. One was the grocer and the other was the cop."

Pat shook her head. "Please. Not the cop."

"Right, not the cop. Although for a while I wasn't too sure about that." Tony signaled for a right turn, ready to ease off the highway and onto the loop leading to the Musket Beach access road along the slope of Mount Kenai.

"Anyway. As I was saying, I started worrying about that remark of Taylor's: 'A wife can cause a lot of trouble.' Maybe he was referring to *my* wife. To you!"

He reached over to pat her leg, then left his hand there, lifting and dropping his thumb as he made his points.

"Taylor knew your name—someone in Musket Beach must have told him.

"He left Hollywood in a hurry, running out on some very important and high-paying recording sessions— maybe that 'someone' also told him that you were snooping around his house.

"Then I found out that Taylor was flying his own plane back to Musket Beach—that's when I really got concerned and came home."

She put her hand over his. "Thank you."

He gave her leg one more rub. "Nada."

Then he took his hand away and turned onto Cedar Street, looking for Paul Taylor's house.

"What a site!" was Tony's reaction driving over the big block numerals on Taylor's blacktop driveway and up the slope to his house. "And he owns all that land around it?"

"So I've heard."

At the top of the drive Tony stopped the car and looked out over his left shoulder at the sweeping, spectacular view down to the town, the beach, the surf, and the sunny blue Pacific Ocean. "Marvelous. I think I can see Maui." He turned the other way, hunching forward and down to see past Pat to the thick dark forest and then through the windshield to the meadow sloping up toward Mount Kenai. "No wonder he doesn't want to sell, if Barrett's rumor is true." He lifted his foot off the brake pedal to let the car roll forward again. "What's back here?"

Sitting up straight, looking around, Pat for some reason spoke very quietly. "Don't know. When I was here before, I parked in front." She craned forward, tense, as they rolled slowly along the blacktop arc and around to the back of the house. "Looks like more driveway. And it looks as though he's home, too. There's a car. I can see the bumper."

They came side-to-side with a two-tone Dodge Dart from the late '70s, its paint flat and dull from salt air and sun. A large dent in the left rear fender was covered with rust the color of dried blood.

"Wait a minute!" she said, her voice low and tight. "That's Martin Ross' car!"

Tony leaned forward, chest against the steering wheel, and studied the old Dodge. "Really? How do you know that?"

"I told you. Remember? He drove up and down the road past the cabin two or three times while you were gone."

"Ah, that's right."

Pat sat back. "Wonderful," she said softly, with more than a little sarcasm.

Like Pat's, Tony's voice, too, was very subdued. "I didn't *think* that was a Taylor-type car."

"Why do you say that?"

"I just don't see him going from a Rolls Corniche in Hollywood to a beach bum special in Musket Beach." Tony pushed back from the wheel, easing the brake a little and letting the Volvo move forward again, slowly. "Wonder what Ross is doing here?"

He looked to his right, past the Dodge and the edge of the blacktop and up the slope. "And I wonder where the garage is?"

"There!" Pat pointed left as they came to the corner of the house. An open two-car garage jutted from its side. The roof of the garage held a small playground— a redwood deck with padded chairs and lounges, a propane gas barbecue, and a hot tub, protected from the wind by tall glass walls.

Almost swallowed by deep shadows, a Volvo SE-1800 station wagon squatted inside the garage, revealed only by narrow strips of outside light reflecting off its chrome-trimmed tail fins.

"Now *there* is a Taylor-type car," Tony said. He tapped Pat on the knee. "And I'd bet that *that's* the car we saw drive away from the beach the other night. A very distinctive design." He smiled grimly, opening his door. "My guess is that your guess was right: Barrett didn't follow it because he knew who was in it and where it was going." Laughing, he added, "And I'll bet that he didn't say anything about it because he thinks it's none of our business!"

Pat didn't smile back as she watched him get out of the car. "I'm glad that you're glad but what are you doing?" She released her seat belt and let it slide through her fingers to rewind on its reel.

Standing by the open door Tony said, "I'm going to look at that car . . ."

Hurrying, nervous, Pat opened the door on her side. "Remember what you said: 'That's what *policemen* are for!'"

". . . and then I'm going to talk to Taylor for a couple of minutes." As he turned toward the garage, Pat's worried cry came across the top of their car. "Tony-y-y!"

As soon as she said it, a pitch-perfect echo came out of the shadows inside the garage. "Tony-y-y!"

Pat hurried around the car and Tony moved to meet her. Standing side-by-side, holding hands, they

203

peered into the dark, then Tony said loudly, "Is that you, Paul?"

Immediately came another pitch-perfect echo, this time in Tony's voice. "That's me, Paul?"

Taylor appeared slowly out of the darkness, wearing a Navy watchcap, peacoat, dungarees, and white sneakers. His long, thick trunk and broad shoulders made him seem much taller than he actually was. His red hair was more tousled than Tony remembered, his beard ruffled. His left hand gestured, his right stayed in the peacoat pocket as he said in his deep natural voice, "Tony Pratt. And this must be Pat. Welcome."

Pat started to nod hello but caught herself.

Tony gestured toward the beat-up Dodge, then toward the low, sporty Volvo in the garage. "Interesting combination of cars," he said.

Taylor smiled brightly. "Yes, it is. Well . . ."

For the first time since Tony had met him, the glib little actor seemed at a loss for words.

Then, as if finding his place in a script, he started again and finished with a rush. "Well, that, uh—that old wagon's still good for beer runs and towing the boat trailer."

He began a friendly chuckle but cut it off when Pat inhaled sharply and raised her eyebrows.

Tony squeezed her hand a little, looking at the car's rear bumper, then at Taylor. "Must be a tricky towing rig. I don't see a trailer hitch."

Taylor's broad smile tightened a little and his voice lost its fake-cheerful edge. "So you noticed that, huh?"

"And that car looks a lot like the one Martin Ross drives."

The smile began to fade. The voice deepened. "Noticed that, too."

Taylor pulled his right hand slowly out of the peacoat pocket. A blood-stained handkerchief covered his knuckles. His fingers were wrapped around a small silver pistol, aimed at Tony. "C'm'ere," he said quietly, wincing as he wagged the pistol.

Tony moved forward, holding Pat's hand.

"Both of you, that's right. You might as well come in, too. Of course, if I had known that *all* of you were coming I'd have arranged for a caterer. And a small but tasteful band."

Taylor cradled his bandaged right hand in his left and wiggled both hands toward the interior of the garage. "Inside and upstairs."

Still holding hands, Tony and Pat stumbled through the dark garage, then up the wooden stairs and into the clean, colorful yellow kitchen.

"Hold it!" Taylor followed them into the kitchen and stopped. Agitated, shaking his head, pointing the gun at Tony then at Pat then back again he said, "Everybody talks about the Hollywood crazies, but I'm tellin' you, man, per capita, you've got more fruitcakes right here in little old Musket Beach than there are in all of California!"

Taylor took a deep breath and in the pause Tony said, "You're changing the subject quite a bit. We were talking about cars."

"No, same subject! That car!—" pointing out the

window toward Martin Ross' car "—belongs to that fruitcake!—" pointing down the hallway "—that I've got locked up in there!"

Pat stared at him. "You mean Martin Ross?"

Taylor tapped his temple four times, in rhythm with the syllables as he said, "Tap-i-o-ca. That's what he's got for brains." He tapped his head once more. "Tapioca! I even had to belt the old fart! *I* never belt anybody!"

He looked down at his injured hand, paused, then leered at Pat and wiggled his eyebrows in Groucho Marx fashion. "That's my lovin' hand, too."

"Where *is* Ross?" Tony asked. "Is he all right?"

"Of course he's all right! Except that he's out of his gourd." Taylor flicked his hand at Pat and said accusingly, "And *you*, of *all* people, ought to *know* he's a ding-a-ling. He told me on the phone about following you around, scared that you'd find out something about him and his big scheme."

He waved his gun toward the doorway. "Go on," he ordered. "Through there. I'll show you."

Between teal walls they walked to a crossing hallway and turned right. On their left was the double-paned glass of Taylor's studio. He opened a door on the right. Inside was a tidy, well-organized equipment closet with tape reels, spools, cords, jacks, and other recording gear neatly stored on racks, hooks, and shelves. In the middle of all this sat Martin Ross, strapped to a secretary chair.

Ross had a wad of tissues stuffed in his mouth and held in place with gaffer's tape. More of the silver, two-inch-wide tape was wrapped around his thighs, holding him to the chair, and around his wrists, binding his arms behind him.

Slumped over his paunch the grocer looked older, grayer. His glasses were in place, but his hair was mussed. Blood seeped from a cut in the left corner of his mouth. His polyester shirt, jacket, and pants were wrinkled and twisted under the tape.

Ross looked up. His eyes, slitted against the sudden light, slowly opened wide, surprised at the sight of Tony and Pat. He glanced quickly back and forth between them several times before he caught a glimpse of the shining silver gun in Taylor's hand. Tears filled his eyes, rolling slowly from the corners, damming up where his glasses met his cheeks, spilling around and down making crooked wet trails through his day-old gray beard. With his wet sad eyes focused on Tony and Pat, Ross shook his head gently from side to side.

Taylor was calm, matter-of-fact. "The old fart is a fruitcake, I tell you."

Odd, muffled sounds came from the grocer's throat as he tried to speak.

"I'll bet he's *still* saying that I killed Carl Conley."

Taylor stepped forward between the Pratts, directly in front of Ross, and raised the small silver pistol to hip level.

Pat looked at him in surprise and said, almost in a whisper, "You? Killed Conley?"

She got no response.

Ross looked around fearfully, shivering.

Taylor suddenly backed out into the hallway, waggling the gun. "Get him outta there! Roll him outta there! Into the studio! Let's get some room!"

Tony stepped around behind Ross' chair and wheeled it out of the closet, following Pat following the little actor as he walked backwards down the short hallway toward his studio. Coming to the door, Taylor held it open and kicked the doorstop into place. The others moved past him into the fifteen-by-fifteen-foot room; he followed them inside.

Pat stopped in the center of the studio. As she turned back toward the door, she glanced toward the window at the tape recording machine with the scuffed spot on top where an editing block had once been attached.

Tony wheeled Martin Ross to Pat's left side and slightly behind her, then stepped forward, to Ross' left. They all watched the little man with the gun.

Taylor stood by the door holding the pistol waist-high, looking at Ross. Then he stepped quickly over to Tony. "Here," he said, disgusted. "Take this thing!" Holding the gun in his open hand, Taylor looked down at the floor and shook his head. "That clown's got me so freaked out I don't know what the hell I'm doing!"

Tony reached out and carefully palmed the gun, fingers around the trigger guard. Taylor watched, and when the gun was out of his hand he stretched his arms out wide and shrugged his shoulders, laughing, "I don't even know how to handle one of those things."

Tony's head and shoulders jerked back. Surprised,

he said, "Why own a gun if you don't know how to use it?"

"Not my gun, man," Taylor said. He waved his bloody right hand at Ross. "Belongs to the grocery man, man. I took it way from him earlier this morning, when he came charging in here like a fucking maniac." The little actor caught his breath, embarrassed. He glanced quickly at Pat and bowed his head. "You should pardon the expression 'maniac.'"

TWENTY-FOUR

Earlier That Day—
Taylor's Flashback

As Taylor told Tony and Pat, at seven-thirty that morning he'd been sitting in his kitchen, drinking coffee and talking on the telephone to a New York advertising agency about the tapes he'd re-recorded in Los Angeles.

He said he finished his call and, as he was hanging up the phone, he glanced out the window and there was Martin Ross parking his rusty old Dodge at the back of the house. He watched Ross squeeze his stubby little form out of the car and scurry across the blacktop, shooting nervous glances all around, as if he were afraid that someone might be watching. Well, someone was.

Inside, Taylor hurried over to his kitchen door. Up the back steps came the grocer. Just as he grabbed for the doorknob, Taylor jerked the door open. Ross almost tumbled into the room but he threw out his hands and grabbed the door frame. Taylor stepped in front of him. "What are you after, grocery man?" Taylor sneered. "What is it this time? Got another real estate con?"

Ross glared at him. "We've got to talk, you and me! We got to settle all this." He straightened himself up and brushed at the sparse gray hair splayed over his head, scraped the fingers of his right hand across the stubble on his cheeks, blinked his red-rimmed, bloodshot eyes.

"That's the same song you played when you called me at the studio in L.A. And I'll tell you now what I told you then." Taylor was still sneering. "We've got nothing to talk about—nothing to settle. So get off it! Go home and get some rest, man. You look awful."

He started to close the door but Ross shoved a foot out and blocked it with his boot. His hands flitted nervously to his hair, his glasses, his jacket pockets, his fly.

"Look," Taylor said, "I've got some recording to do, so . . ." He tried again to close the door but the boot stopped it.

The grocer's voice was harsh and tight, grating as he said, "Don't tell *me* we got nothin' to talk about. Carl Conley's dead. And I know you killed him and . . ."

"You're out of your tree, pops . . ." Taylor relaxed his hold on the door and turned away, seeming to miss Ross' next words.

They were just a faint croak. "And now you've made *me* do it, too." Stepping across the door sill, Ross pulled a small silver pistol out of his back pocket.

Taylor turned back to Ross. "What're you talking

about, grocery man? Made you do wha . . ." Taylor saw
the gun and his eyes widened and his face turned pale
behind his beard. He laughed a shaky, nervous laugh.
"Hey. Don't point that thing at me, man!" He backed
away, toward the corner where the entry hall met the
hallway to his studio.

Ross kept moving forward, talking, not hearing. "It's
got to get over and done with. You ruined that poor girl.
And that marriage. And then you killed her husband.
But you won't stop *me*."

Even though he was backing away from a gun
pointed at his belly, Taylor's instincts took over—either
his actor's training or his own combative nature made
him try to take control. His head jerked back and he
yelled, "Ruined *what* poor girl, grocery man? *What*
marriage!" His back bumped into the corner and he
stopped. With his thick shoulders he pushed off the wall
toward Ross but the gun came up, aimed between his
eyes, and he leaned back. His voice turned quiet but
stayed quick and angry, and his shoulders moved as he
swung his arms and he slapped the back of his right
hand into his left palm, over and over.

"That wasn't a marriage! Anybody could see that!
Same old story: 'Hot little country girl meets older guy.
Marries him for money. The money runs out. Phffft,
she's gone.' So don't give me any shit about 'marriage,'
grocery man. That broad'll roll over for anybody with
a glass of wine and a smile."

Ross' bloodshot eyes squeezed shut. His lips
quivered. "No more," he whispered.

"But you knew all that!" Taylor raged on, apparently missing those soft words. "You just wanted Conley to work me over for your screwball real estate deal and …" He stopped, his big bearded head cocked to one side. He seemed to be listening. After a moment, calmer, he said, "Wait a minute. What do you mean, 'No more'?"

Ross rubbed a hand across his face, hard. He blinked several times and took a deep breath. In a hoarse voice he said, "Move. Down there," waving his gun toward the hall.

Backing into the short hallway Taylor blurted out, "Come on! What do you mean, 'No more'!"

Ross stopped at the studio door and motioned toward it with the gun.

"In here. Where you killed Carl."

Walking backwards into his studio, Taylor shoved his arms at the ceiling and rolled his head back and yelled, "I did *not* kill Conley, grocery man! For chrissakes how many times do I have to *say* that!"

Taylor stopped when his backside bumped the console table. He glanced quickly behind him and his eyes flashed with a sudden idea when he saw the lights glowing in the dials on the mixing console and the remote control panel; earlier, before going out to the kitchen to make that telephone call, he'd turned the console on and cued-up some tapes. Now a music tape for playback and a blank tape for recording were all cued and ready to go.

Turning back to Ross, Taylor's body sagged and his hands flopped down against the sides of his legs and he said wearily, "Conley died because of a stupid accident. He took a punch at me. I hit him in the gut and pushed

214

him away. He *fell.* He hit his head on that recording machine." Taylor pointed to the Scully tape machine under the window, taking a quick look to make sure that its lights were on and the music reel was ready for playback.

"You killed him . . ."

"It was an *accident!*"

Ross' voice began to rise. ". . . and now you've told *her* about it."

Taylor straightened. His eyes were brighter and he almost smiled when he said, "So that's how you know." He nodded, relaxing a little against he console, folding his arms. "Yes, I told her. Flying back from L.A. What the hell, she didn't give a damn about Carl Conley. I knew that. So I told her." He shrugged. "Anyway, it was an accident." There was an actor's pause and his voice got hard. "And I also told her that she was a girl with a lot of problems, that I don't need girls with problems, and so we wouldn't be seeing each other anymore."

Holding the gun steady, Ross spoke softly, his eyes almost closed. "That's what she told me. When she called me yesterday."

Taylor shook his head. "No, no. She was in L.A. yesterday. With me. Don't you remember? You tried to call her. At the studio." He slapped his forehead, exasperated. "And why I gave her that number, and why *she gave it to you,* I'll never know. But you talked to *me* yesterday. Remember, grocery man? Remember telling me about scaring the Pratt broad to keep her from snooping around here?"

It was Ross' turn to shake his head. "Later. She

215

called me later. After you got back from L.A. After you drove from the airport to her place. She called from the motel. By the Sand Castle beach." Ross spoke in short bursts, as if reciting half-remembered bits of a memorized speech. His voice dropped, tired, at the end of each fragment. His dark, red-circled eyes seemed hypnotized, staring at Taylor. "She called. Wanted me to meet her on the beach. Behind the motel. Late. Nobody around. She wanted help. Wanted to get back at you."

"Get back at *me*? Because of Conley? You've got to be kidding!"

Taylor moved forward a step and Ross' eyes were suddenly alert. "Stay there!"

The little actor stepped back, but now he was in a slightly different position. Just behind him, on his right, was the end of the mixing console, with remote control buttons to operate the tape machine by the window.

"What are you saying, grocery man? That she wanted to get back at me because of Conley?"

"No. Because you didn't go for the real estate deal me and Carl worked up: You'd sell your land here to me, then I'd sell it to the guru and his people." Ross shook his head slowly, sadly. "Money. The things we do for money." He shook his head again. "When she saw that Carl couldn't get you to go for it, she said *she* could get you to sell your property. And she wanted lotsa money for doin' it. And then she wanted half the money *I'd* make when I sold it to the guru's crowd."

Taylor rubbed his chin whiskers and laughed.

216

"Gotta give her credit for thinking big. This property's worth a couple of million bucks and more." His right hand dropped behind his back. "But she'd never get me to sell. Never."

"That's what I told her, after you turned Carl down time and time again. But she said if I didn't give her money to work on you, she'd go to the police—tell 'em how Carl died and swear I was behind the whole thing, maybe even that *I* killed Carl. Said she was gonna go find Barry Barrett. Right now." Ross fell back into tired, fragmented speech again. "And she started to go. Toward the motel. The motel coffee shop. Barrett was in there. Drinkin' coffee. Oregon state trooper, too."

Taylor's right hand moved behind his back, slowly, feeling for the remote control buttons at the edge of the console. Ross blinked and glared at him, hard, and his hand paused.

Ross' voice began to rise. "I couldn't let her do that, could I? Spoil everything?" He spoke as if asking for understanding. "Ruin my chance to get the guru's people to buy land here? Throw away all the building contracts? The jobs? The *business* at stake for Musket Beach? Lose a chance to bring this town some recognition from all over the *state*?" With his free hand, Ross reached up and tried to smooth his hair into place, then shoved a forefinger under his glasses and rubbed tears out of his eyelashes.

His gun sagged toward the floor, but Ross stopped and took a deep breath and brought it back up again, aimed at Taylor's chest. When Ross went on, his voice

217

was soft, nearly a whisper, and grainy, and his damp eyes narrowed, watching Taylor but looking through him to another place. "We were down there by the motel. By the Sand Castle beach. She started to leave— to go tell Barrett. To ruin me. I grabbed her arm. She jerked away and my hand took hold of her neck and she started to scream and I choked it off and she fell down and pulled me on top of her and all of a sudden I had *both* hands on her neck and I couldn't stop." He took another breath. "Couldn't stop."

A tear slid down his cheek along the right side of Ross' nose. He raised his forefinger again and scrubbed at the left side. He blinked several times and looked out the window and then quickly back.

Taylor's hand was moving slowly behind his back, palm-down on the remote control buttons. The Stop button was under the heel of his palm. Then came Start, then Rewind, and then, under his fingertips, the convex button marked Record.

Watching Ross, Taylor asked quietly, "And then what?"

As he answered, Ross flexed his fingers around the pistol butt and opened his eyes wide. "And then I buried her in the sand." He pointed the gun barrel steadily at Taylor's chest. "And now I guess I'll have to bury you someplace."

Behind his back, Taylor's middle finger pressed the Rewind button. The switch clicked and made contact and Ross' eyes flickered toward the tape machine standing alone by the window. Its gears engaged and—

as if by magic—the silent, unattended reels started turning backwards.

Ross jerked his head around and glared at the machine, stunned, as the reels began spinning faster and faster.

With his left hand Taylor flipped up the volume control all the way and suddenly the small room shook with sound, with the eerie, piercing shriek of singers and orchestra playing backwards at high speed. Out of the loudspeakers cranked up to full volume the strange, madhouse noise screamed down at Ross. He'd never heard anything like it, never imagined, never dreamed it. Never in his worst and wildest nightmare had he ever conceived and suffered such a loud loud frightening inhuman noise. His face turned dead gray, his jaw slopped open, his scared startled eyes rolled at the insane, pulsing, unstoppable screech that beat at him from somewhere in this strange, crazy room. He jerked his head up looking frantically left and right trying to find the ear-shattering sound and Taylor's left foot kicked the gun out of his hand and his right fist smashed into the corner of Ross' open mouth.

Ross staggered back and fell against the door frame and sagged slowly to the floor, squeezing his eyes shut, mashing his hands over his ears, curling into a fat gray ball trying to hide from the frightening skin-crawling shattering noise and from everything else that was going wrong.

TWENTY·FIVE

Saturday Afternoon— Taylor's House

AFTER he finished telling the story of his morning with Martin Ross—dramatizing it, really—Paul Taylor blew out a big breath. He let his shoulders droop, as if the telling had used up all his energy. He turned his back to Tony and Pat, and to Ross.

Ross still sat in the center of the studio, his arms moving quietly against the wide gray tape that strapped him to a chair. His head hung down, but his eyes glared over the top of his glasses at Taylor, cold and hard.

Tony stood near Ross and let the little silver gun dangle from his right hand as he studied the grocer. "I have the feeling," he said to Taylor, "that Ross is not happy that you told us that story."

Pat nodded. "Especially not with him in the same room."

Taylor shrugged. "Tough tacos."

Pat had been resting a hip against the counter beside the mixing console, but now she moved around Tony to Ross' other side. "And does he have to stay gagged like that? Why don't we at least take the tape off his face?"

Seeming to forget the fear and worry that he'd caused in the last few days, she began carefully pulling the tape away from Ross' mouth as Taylor leaned on the now-silent tape machine, arms stiff, tipping his head from side to side and tapping his fingers on the machine as he summed up his main points. "So anyway: that's how I got the grocery man all taped up, how I got the sore knuckles, how I got the gun you're holding—and that's pretty much the whole ravioli."

At that moment, Officer Barrett spoke from the open studio doorway, "No, Mr. Taylor, I'm afraid you and I still have a few things to talk about."

Taylor straightened and spun around. His face showed surprise, first, then chagrin, and then good humor as he bounced the heel of his hand lightly off his forehead. "But I'm *always* aware of my audience!" he said with a laugh. "So how did I miss you? How long have you been there?"

"Long enough to know that you and I're gonna have some pretty serious discussions about some pretty serious charges."

Officer Barrett hooked his thumbs casually over his belt buckle and sauntered into the room, elbows and shoulders moving loosely. The same Trooper Kelsey who had been with him on the beach now took Barrett's place in the doorway.

Barrett stopped behind Martin Ross. "We can talk about how Carl Conley died, for example," Barrett continued. "And, if he died here, we can talk about how he got moved from here to the beach. And we can talk about that little metal block that Mr. and Mrs. Pratt found on the beach by the body." Barrett paused. "We can also talk about a charge of manslaughter, or possibly even murder."

Taylor chuckled and said, "Oh, come now, Officer ..." He paused, holding his voice on an upward inflection as if trying to remember his lines.

"Barrett," Pat said, prompting him. "Officer Barrett."

Taylor was all actor, now, beaming her a big smile and a short bow. "Thank you, Mrs. Pratt. Thank you."

He began pacing in front of the tape recorder, looking back to Barrett, smiling, giving the appearance of being in control, his voice deep and confident.

"Well, as I guess you heard when you were in the hall, there *was* an accident here. Yes. Carl Conley *did* die here. Accidentally, if I may repeat myself. He and I had a little disagreement. Not a fight. Perhaps an altercation but definitely not a fight. And he fell. He hit his head against the top of this tape machine. He hit it so hard that the editing block came loose and it fell on the floor."

Taylor paused. "I'll admit," he said with a sweeping motion of his bandaged right hand and a bob of his

223

head, "I'll admit that dumping Conley on the beach was not the smartest move anybody ever made. And I don't know why I had that editing block in my pocket. Or how I dropped it."

The little actor was the center of attention and he made the most of it. He paused again, smoothing his hair with his good hand, stroking his beard.

"All I know is that I was terribly confused, mixed up, angry, and in a great hurry. A studio in Hollywood had just called and I had to get down there as soon as possible to re-record some sound tracks that're scheduled on the networks on Monday night. So I had a mountain of things to do."

He began pacing in front of the tape machine, four steps left and four steps back, smacking his hands together as he monotonously ticked off his chores.

"I had to get to Seashore, gas up my plane, file a flight plan, and so on and so on. So, I'm running around here, packing a bag and trying to get ready for this hurry-up trip to L.A. and BOOM! All of a sudden: *Conley's* back! He prances in here doing his 'leading man' act—the 'star' of the Musket Beach Little Theater, for chrissakes—a skinny Willy Loman trying to sell me some cockamamie real estate idea that *this* fruitcake ..."

Taylor, pointing to Ross, stopped, and snapped his fingers, slapped his hands together like an old-time vaudeville pitchman and said, "You wanta know how this whole thing started? *I'll* tell you how this whole thing started," and he turned around to his other tape machine, the one that he'd loaded with blank tape earlier in the day, before Ross appeared.

While he talked, Taylor's hands moved quickly over the mixing console and the tape machine, rewinding the reel, turning down the volume, adjusting speeds, stopping the tape expertly just before it hit the silent leader. "You're in for a treat, ladies and gentlemen, something that I almost forgot—a 'live,' in-person, first-nand, on-the-spot confession from Mr. Martin Ross himself."

Taylor pointed to Ross. Pat had pulled most of the tape off his face but his mouth was still stuffed with tissues, so all he could do was look and grunt questions at Taylor.

"The grocery man didn't even know he was being recorded—he's never been in a studio before—he didn't know when I turned the mike on—and I sat in front of the tape machine so he couldn't see the reels turning.

"After things calmed down in here, after I finally got the grocery man wrapped up as you see him now—except for the gag, of course—we had a quiet little talk."

Suddenly, Ross jerked upright, grunting at Taylor, shaking his head violently.

Officer Barrett said loudly, "Hold it, Martin! Let's hear this!"

Ross slumped back again, watching Taylor. Veins stood out in his neck and throat, and tears filled his eyes, tears either of rage or sorrow.

225

Taylor turned around to the tape machine, punched the Play button, and out of the speakers came his own voice, quiet and restrained.

TAYLOR: Listen, grocery man, you know I'm gonna call the cops, right?

Ross: Suppose so. Yeah.

TAYLOR: But before I do that, would you—just to satisfy my own curiosity—can you tell me how you got mixed up in this whole ridiculous schemozzle.

Ross: What?

TAYLOR: How did this thing get started?

(A LONG PAUSE)

Ross: In the store, a couple of months ago, a guy from one of those religious outfits comes in—the ones in the blue robes?

TAYLOR: The Krishnas?

Ross: No. But you get the idea. The head guy in this outfit is called The Loved One. Anyway, one of those people comes in and while he's at the cash register he wants to know if I know of any property for sale in Musket Beach. So I told him to go see Carl Conley. "Best real estate man in town," I said. The truth of it is, Carl didn't know his ass from a cedar stump. But I thought him and that guru fella oughta get along just great, both being actors of a sort. What I mean is, anybody that calls himself a "guru" and wants people to think he's got all the answers has got to be dealing pretty heavy in horse manure. As for Conley—well, any grown man that

226

gets up on a "little theater" stage every weekend and pretends to be somebody else, I say he's a little out o' plumb. So, I figured I'd sic those two phonies on each other and that'd be the end of it. But a couple o' weeks later Carl comes up to me on Main Street and says he wants to give me a "finders fee" out of the great big commission he's gonna make out of the guru's bunch. Says they're gonna spend a *million dollars* or more for a piece of land here in Musket Beach. A million dollars.

(A LONG PAUSE ON THE TAPE)

Right then, I reckon, is where my head started to go wrong. Anyway, Carl said the guru's crowd wanted to buy all this property of yours ...

TAYLOR: And I told Conley he was crazy!

ROSS: That's what *I* said.

TAYLOR: I'm not selling my house, my land, or any combination thereof.

ROSS: He figured the million dollars would talk you into it. And if that didn't work, he figured his wife—well, that's how screwy I got with all that money talk: Not only was I listening to Carl Conley, but I didn't say one word against it when he talked about lettin' his wife—well, everybody in town knew about you and her. What I'm saying is, he even *encouraged* it, hoping that she could get you to change your mind.

(ANOTHER LONG SILENCE.)

And what's worse, Lord save us, I went along with it.

TAYLOR: "Money is the root of all evil," as the Bible says.

Ross: No. What the Bible says is, "The *love* of money
is the root of all evil." First Book of Timothy.
(ANOTHER, LONGER SILENCE ON THE TAPE. PAT,
TONY, AND THE OTHERS IN THE STUDIO WAITED,
STARING AT THE REELS TURNING ROUND AND
ROUND, LISTENING TO THE SMALL SOUND OF
THE MOTOR AND THE FAINT SQUEAKS OF THE
TAPE REELS UNTIL ROSS'S SAD, SUBDUED VOICE
CONTINUED.)

It's true. Evil. And going crazy. I know. The money
was all I could think about: How much those people
would spend for land, for housing two thousand
"disciples," for equipment and tools and food. I
thought about how good it would be for Musket
Beach, and pretty soon that's *all* I was thinkin
about. Turned me as nutty as Carl Conley. I started
playing games: In private, I was sneaking around
like a thief to meet Conley in secret, pushing him
to keep after you to sell. But in public, I pretended
to hate him and the guru, and let on that it didn't
bother me that his wife was fooling around with
you.

(ONCE MORE, SILENCE.)

Drove me crazy. A crazy thief that's what I turned
into. A crazy thief that condoned another man
urging his wife's adultery . . . Lordy, lordy. We're
all weak, I know, but I never thought I could fall
so low. It's like I'm another person. Out of control
It's not me.

(ROSS CHOKED BACK A SOB.)

* * *

Everyone in the studio stared at the reels turning slowly, around and around, waiting for another voice from the tape to break the silence. Instead, it was Pat who suddenly screamed, "Tony, look out! Ross—!"

Martin Ross, tears streaming down his cheeks from his sad and empty eyes, had worked his raw, bleeding wrists free of the tape around his arms. He snatched the gun out of Tony's hand and tried to stand. His legs and shoulders were still strapped to the chair but somehow he got to his feet, staggering, grotesquely hunched over, the chair taped to his back with its wheels spinning in the air. Growling and groaning through the tissues stuffed in his mouth, the little round grocer staggered across the room, pointing his gun at the terrified Taylor.

The pistol cracked and a bullet whined off the tape machine and shattered the window.

Tony grabbed Pat and ducked behind the console Barrett and the trooper shook off their surprise and lunged at Ross as the pistol cracked once, twice more Taylor's expression froze. Two small red holes had popped out on his chest and his belly and he grunted at each hit. He grunted again and pushed away from the tape machine to break Ross' weird charge.

Lowering his head, he grabbed the grocer in a violent bear hug just as Barrett and the trooper reached out to pull them apart. Taylor's impact and his fierce, strong hug forced the pistol back into Ross and it fired again, this time soft and muffled. Taylor let go of Ross

229

The policemen stepped back. Ross and the chair rattled to the floor.

Taylor stood for a moment, pale, shaking, his stubby body weaving over Ross. Softly, he massaged the hole in the belly of his peacoat with his trembling left hand. It came away red. Holding both hands out, he studied the bloody fingers of his left hand and the blood-soaked bandage around his right knuckles. Looking between his hands he stared down at Martin Ross. "Fruitcake," he whispered. "Total fruitcake." And he fell.

TWENTY·SIX

Saturday Evening—
The Cabin

SITTING on the couch in the cabin, Pat had her sneakers up on the hatch-cover coffee table. Her back and shoulders pressed deep into the couch cushions. With both hands she clutched a tall glass of J&B and water, its ice nearly melted away, the drink nearly untouched. Shaking her head slowly, she was saying, "I never want to see anything like that again!"

On the other side of the table, also feet up, Tony had rocked back in the rocker and was sipping through the beery foam of a Henry's.

"Think of it," Pat went on, "just four days ago . . ." She interrupted herself and looked at Tony, her eyes wide. "Good Lord, was it only four days?"

He lowered his glass and nodded. "Seems impossible, doesn't it?"

She blinked rapidly but her voice was a slow monotone. "Four days. We sat here and stared at that little metal block and I said, 'You sound like a man trying to work out a plot.'"

Officer Barrett snapped his notebook shut and slapped it down on the dining table. "Good thinking," he said loudly.

Tony and Pat turned and looked at him. He leaned back in his chair waving at them with a can of root beer, dipping and wagging his head in agreement. "Very good thinking. You just keep on working on those plots." Then, in a more serious tone, "Let me tell you something. Again. The best advice you ever got, you got from your friendly, neighborhood police officer. That advice is, 'You do your job, and let police officers do theirs.'"

Barrett looked at each of them and said earnestly, "You folks were pretty lucky to come out of this thing all in one piece, y'know. You could've got yourselves hurt pretty bad."

His head tilted back and he drained the rest of the root beer, his Adam's apple sliding up and down in his craned-back neck. Finished, and without moving from his chair, he stretched his body and a long arm across to the counter between the kitchen and the livingroom and stood the empty can beside two others.

"I'll have to admit, though," he added in mid-stretch before relaxing back into his chair. "We have you folks to thank for digging up that connection between Conley and Ross. *And* that crazy scheme to buy Paul Taylor's land and bring that guru and his gang to town."

Barrett's head bowed and he wagged it back and forth. The corner of his mouth jerked as he made a short sucking sound. "Fruitcake is right."

"What *about* Paul Taylor?" Pat asked. "He s still alive, isn't he? Is he going to be all right?"

"Don't know." Barrett shook his head again before he looked up. "The doctor says it's pretty iffy, but there s a good chance he can pull through." Wiping a hand across his lip, smoothing his mustache, he made that sucking sound again and said, "Funny thing. He takes two bullets and he still has a chance. Ross takes one and he's dead before he hits the floor."

Barrett pushed up from his chair, belt and holster squeaking, and pointed his notebook at Tony. "But the big thing for you folks is, take that advice: Leave police work to police officers."

Pat and Tony rose, nodding and looking a little like chastised children, and trailed Barrett to the door.

"One more thing," he said over his shoulder. "The sheriff's people and probably somebody from the State Police in Salem will be wanting to talk to you, too. So let me know if you plan any more traveling."

"Just from here to Portland, and that's all," Pat said, giving Tony a very impressive look. "And back if you need us."

Barrett stepped through the open doorway to the bright sunlight on the front deck. Squinting as he pulled out his sunglasses, he turned and gave Pat a quick half-smile.

"Well, be talkin' to you," he said, holding his hand

out to her. She gave it a firm shake before she asked, "By the way, how did you happen to show up at Taylor's place just when you did?"

Barrett smiled again while he and Tony shook hands. "I knew you wouldn't stay away from there, even after I told you to. So when we got business taken care of with Carole Conley's body—the medical examiner and county people and all—I drove by here, just to check. Your station wagon was gone, so I headed on up to Taylor's. Figured that's where you folks'd be, 'cause you always seem to know where the action is."

He put on his serious face again and once more held up a cautioning hand. "And for your own sakes, I ask you not to do it again. Even if you *do* know where the action is, leave it alone."

The phone rang inside the cabin.

Barrett waved his notebook. "Be talkin' to you," he said once more, and clomped across the deck and down to his car.

Tony stepped back inside the doorway and reached around the lamp to pick up the phone. "Hello?"

"Hey, Tones! 'S that you, babes?" Irwin Jackson's deep rumbling voice was unmistakable, even over the long distance line from Los Angeles.

"Hey, Jax. How's everything going?"

"Everything's cool, babes. Abe is right here, on the other line, and the job is all done and everybody's happy, including The Client, so we called to give you the word."

Abe came on the extension with his pseudo-stern

voice. "Are you going to thank me for saving your ass when you ducked outta here?"

"Thank you for saving my ass when I ducked outta there."

"Your ass is welcome." Abe chuckled. "You had the job almost finished, anyway."

"Well, it's a good idea for somebody from the agency to be there at the end, just in case any problems come up. Thanks for taking over."

"No sweat," Abe said. "But speaking of problems, everything okay with Pat?—or whatever it was that made you duck outta here?"

"Oh, sure. All clear. I'll tell you both all about it, next time I see you."

Jax's eager voice cut in. "When're you coming back, Tones? Got some other jobs lined up down here?"

As Jax spoke, Tony turned around and looked out through the doorway to the front deck where Pat was standing, glass in hand, one foot up on the railing, watching the sea.

"No, nothing else lined up in L.A. right now, Jax. What I have to do now is get back to book-writin'. I've got an outline and three chapters of a new book due before long."

From the deck, Pat looked quickly into the cabin, nodding emphatic approval.

"But there may be a pretty interesting production job coming up in a couple of months."

"Down here?"

"No, here in Oregon. A Japanese television crew is coming over from Tokyo to shoot a series for one of the Japanese TV networks."

"Are you serious?" Abe cut in, laughing. "A Japanese soap opera? Made in Oregon?"

Laughing, too, Tony said, "That's what it sounds like. And somehow they got my name."

Pat straightened and turned her head to look at Tony, staring out of the sunlight and into the deep shadow of the cabin.

Abe's voice came back. "What kind of work can an old ad-agency-copy-guy-and-now-book-writer do for a Japanese TV show?"

"They want me to scout locations, handle local production odds and ends, help audition local talent, things like—"

On the deck, Pat's glass slipped from her fingers, glanced off the top rail and landed, luckily unbroken, in the grass below.

Tony frowned and said quickly, "Listen, Abe. Jax. I've got to go. Thanks for calling, and thanks again for taking care of things after I left."

"No sweat."

"Later, Tones."

Tony dropped the phone onto the cradle and hurried out to Pat. Her wide eyes were still staring at him.

"What's the matter?" he asked, holding his hands out for hers.

She turned and grabbed both of his hands. "A funny feeling," she said softly. "It started when you were

236

talking about a TV crew from Japan." Her voice was strained and very quiet. "For some reason, I hope you don't take that job."

He put his arms around her and they stood together, their two shadows becoming one. "Is something the matter? Do you feel bad?"

She put her head back and looked up at him, frowning, shivering a little in the sunshine. "Cold."

He tried to smile. "You were holding an icy glass."

Her voice was worried, quiet, questioning. "Inside."

Much later, starlight and moonlight seemed to float through the open bedroom window on the sound of the surf. Under the comforter Pat lay on her side, pressed against Tony, a hand on his chest, her head cradled in the hollow of his shoulder, his arms around her.

They had had dinner at The Beach House, just up the highway. Drinks and seafood bisque and steamed clams with saffron rice and a bottle of wine had softened the edges of a hard day. Now they lay together, feeling each other's warmth.

"Long day," he said, sighing.

"Mm-hmmm," Pat hummed, reaching up and kissing his earlobe gently. "We could make it just a little longer." Her hand moved between the first two buttons of his pajama top and her fingers coiled through the hair on his chest.

"I'm sorry to say this," he said quietly, his right hand softly massaging her back, "but I'm sort of tired."

She unbuttoned the first button and her voice was

sympathetic. "That's too bad." She unbuttoned the second.

He cupped the back of her head in his right hand and his fingers caressed behind her ear. "My day started very early in Los Angeles, you know."

She unbuttoned the last button and opened the shirt wide. "Poor thing."

She kissed his chest, her tongue circling one nipple, then the other. Her hand moved slowly around and down and slipped under the waist of his pajama pants. After a moment she raised herself on one elbow, smiling in the moonlight. "You devil, you," she said, "you're not tired at all."